A HURT FOR A HURT

A Dan Ballantine Mystery

Mark Travis

"A Hurt For A Hurt" by Mark Travis. ISBN 978-1-62137-024-6 (softcover).

Library of Congress Control Number: 2012905764

Manufactured in the United States of America.

1

Jeffrey Turner Sanford stepped through the gate at New Folsom Prison into, other than five years of supervised parole, freedom. He stopped, took a deep breath of untainted air, and looked up at a sky not bordered by gray walls and dark towers manned by uniformed guards with high-powered rifles.

A woman shouted, "Jeffrey!"

The young man lowered his eyes, looked westerly, and saw his mother and father standing on the sidewalk next to a shiny black Mercedes SUV. He stepped toward them.

Kimberly Sanford cried as she ran to and hugged her only son.

James stepped closer and shook Jeffrey's free hand. "You look well, son. A little pale, maybe, but the summer sun will fix that."

Jeffrey nodded but said nothing. Prison had taught him to keep his mouth shut.

James and Kimberly attempted to engage their son in conversation as they drove him to their million dollar home in an expensive Sacramento neighborhood.

Jeffrey's terse responses worried them.

As the west garage door lifted, Jeffrey saw his black BMW Z4 parked in the end space.

"I uncovered your car, son," said James, "and drove it to the dealer last week. I had it serviced and detailed for you. It's ready to take you to classes."

After several seconds of silence, Jeffrey said, "Thank you, sir."

A few years ago, thought James Sanford, *it would have been 'Thanks a lot, Dad.'*

Kimberly said, "The summer session starts in three weeks, Jeffrey. I hope I can put a few pounds on you between now and then. You look thin."

James parked the Mercedes in the garage, and the trio entered the house.

The family Golden Retriever, Cappie, growled softly at Jeffrey as he followed Kimberly through the laundry room and into the spacious kitchen.

Jeffrey smiled at the old dog, dropped to his knees, and hugged, petted, and scratched her. "It's me, Cappie. Steal anybody's hat lately?"

As an unnamed puppy, the dog found a little league cap on the floor of Jeffrey's closet and made it her favorite toy.

Cappie's demeanor immediately changed from wary to totally happy, and she wagged her bushy tail and jumped on Jeffrey.

"She probably smelled prison on me," said Jeffrey as he petted and rubbed Cappie.

"She's happy to see you," said Kimberly softly. "We all are."

At ten a.m. twelve mornings later James sat in his downtown office in front of his computer. A CAD program helped him design a science building addition to a local community college.

Kimberly attended a brunch meeting of her garden club.

Jeffrey sat on a leather sofa eating dry granola cereal from a bowl with his fingers and watching *The Charge at Feather River* on The Western Channel. He wondered if Guy Madison or any of the other actors in the early 50s black and white western remained alive.

Cappie suddenly raised her head and looked toward the main door. When the doorbell rang, the dog barked and ran toward the tiled entry way.

Jeffrey placed his bowl on the coffee table, pushed himself to his feet, wiped his fingers on his jeans, and stepped to the door. He pushed Cappie back, ordered her to sit, and opened the door.

The person standing on the *Our Dog Can't Hold His Licker!* mat quickly raised a gloved hand holding a nickel-plated Smith & Wesson Model 34 "kit gun" with a suppressor screwed to the muzzle of the two-inch barrel. When the revolver pointed at Jeffrey's face, the killer pulled the trigger. With a soft *thut,* a twenty-two caliber bullet left the pistol, passed through Jeffrey's right eye, entered his brain, and expended its energy bouncing around inside his skull.

Jeffrey crumpled to the textured tiles.

Cappie resumed barking when the stranger stepped into the house and closed the door. The intruder aimed the pistol at Cappie a few seconds then lowered it when the dog stopped barking and did not attack.

While watching Cappie, the killer slowly removed a glove and extended a naked hand toward the dog.

Cappie stopped barking, sniffed the hand, and wagged her tail.

The killer patted Cappie and scratched under her collar. The dog rotated her head with pleasure.

The killer re-gloved then stepped to Jeffrey's head, pulled a ten-inch section of broken pool cue from a hip pocket, and jammed the stick hard into Jeffrey's right eye socket.

The killer patted Cappie once more, opened the door, stepped onto the mat, closed the door, and walked to a vehicle parked next to a fence at the end of the residential block.

2

Penny and I sat in a small rented boat on Lake Wallowa. I sipped coffee from a travel mug and waited for a record-breaking trout to nibble the fat nightcrawler which I hoped still twisted angrily on my treble hook sixty feet below me. The rising sun had just peeked over the eastern mountains and started to warm us when a ring tone in my jacket pocket disturbed the peace.

My cell phone is normally off and in a drawer in my fifth-wheel travel trailer, my permanent home, except at eight o'clock each Saturday morning when I turn it on for an hour or so. That's when the seven people who have my number might try to reach me with hopes I'm not in a dead zone.

But that particular Wednesday morning in late August I still considered myself on a job.

The previous Monday afternoon I sat on the back of a friend's Harley-Davidson Road King. We rode along a graveled drive toward a private home in Joseph, Oregon, a tiny town five miles north of Lake Wallowa. As we neared the front porch, I photographed a "dead" man and his pals. Until we interrupted them, they had sat drinking beers and watching the sun set.

They had also been enjoying the benefits of a three million dollar life insurance policy to which they were not entitled.

Earlier that day I had watched the trio ride their Street Glides onto the property when they returned from a week-long trip to the annual Sturgis, South Dakota, motorcycle rally.

I had transmitted the photographs to Ed Logan in Los Angeles within an hour of taking them. Logan owns and runs an independent insurance adjustment business, and he occasionally asks me to investigate suspected insurance fraud. If I find adequate proof of same, I get ten percent of whatever I save the insurance company that issued the policy.

While I would soon enjoy a nice pay day, I don't consider myself wealthy. At least not in terms of money. My bank, at my direction, sends the Livingston Residential School for the Severely Autistic two thousand dollars per month. My son, Dan Troop Ballantine, Junior, resides there and learns words, numbers, and self-control at a glacial pace. His mother, my former spouse, sends zero dollars.

My retired Road King owning friend who tells strangers he is Horatio Aloysius Gahzertenblatz III, had left our camp the previous afternoon bound for his Reno home. I chose to stay a few more days because I enjoyed the setting, I hoped for that record breaking trout, and, more important, I expected a local lawman to contact me. The 'dead' guy and his pals had been committing felony insurance fraud, and I expected the cops might want to know how I found the trio.

Ed Logan had welcomed my good news. He assured me he would stop the six thousand dollar monthly annuity payments he had been making to two of the three felons. He would also forward my report and photographs to the District Attorney in Marin County, California, who had jurisdiction over the fraud.

Based on my police experience, I estimated that official would take at least three days to review the report, file felony complaints, and issue arrest warrants for the three thirty-something men.

I looked at my phone expecting to see a local number, and I'm sure my face registered surprise to see *Kyra* on the small screen.

Ms. Kyra Simmons, Ph.D., a child psychologist, works three days a week in her private Reno office and two days a week at the Livingston School where her daughter resides. That two days pays for her daughter's room, board, and education.

I can count on one hand, thumb, pinky, and ring finger excluded, the number of times Kyra has telephoned me in the few years I have known her. Because Kyra does not want a husband or a clingy man near her, we enjoy one of those rare 'friends with benefits' relationships. When I'm not working for Ed Logan, I travel the western states from lake to lake towing and living from my trailer. I visit Reno to see my son every two or three weeks, and, on the Wednesday prior to most visits, I call Kyra and ask for a dinner date. These meetings often end with conversation, wine, and music in her condo's living room followed by a visit to her bedroom.

Because Kyra prefers to sleep and wake alone, I always leave by midnight.

I opened my phone and brought it to my face. "Kyra," I said, "what a pleasant surprise. How are you?"

"I'm the one who is surprised, Dan. I assumed your phone would be off, and I would leave a message."

"I found and reported the man I told you about two weeks ago," I said, "and I'm expecting a call from a local law enforcement officer."

"Where is 'local'?"

"I'm camped near Joseph, Oregon."

"I don't recognize that name."

"It's a small town in the northeast corner of the state near the south end of Hell's Canyon."

"Will you be passing through Reno soon? I would like to see you."

I heard tension in her voice. "Is something wrong, Kyra? I could be there late tonight if necessary."

"There's no hurry, Dan," said Kyra. "If you finish your business, we could have dinner Saturday night."

"I will be there. May I knock on your door at seven?"

"You may. Thanks, Dan. See you then."

"Good-bye, Kyra."

I closed my phone and looked at my forty pound mutt. "Screw the local deputy, Penny girl. My fair damsel beckons, and I must travel thither."

3

"My brother died three months ago."

Kyra spoke those words a few seconds after I had commenced chewing a bite of buttered sour dough bread which had followed half a four-cheese ravioli.

My chewing covered the mild shock I felt and gave me time to choose my words.

"I'm sorry, Kyra," I said as I reached for my wine glass. "I didn't know you had a brother." I sipped and added, "And I'm wondering why you did not tell me of your loss before now."

"Jeffrey and I weren't close. You were out of town when my parents called with the bad news, and I drove to Sacramento to attend his funeral." Kyra sipped merlot and looked at me over the top of her glass.

Kyra had mentioned her parents in a previous conversation. I recalled they resided in Sacramento, and her father had a small architectural firm. Kyra said her mother, Kimberly, did not work at anything beyond raising fragrant flowers in her home garden.

She had opened the topic, and I assumed she wanted to discuss it. "How did Jeffrey die?" I asked.

"Jeffrey was four years younger than me," said Kyra as she lowered her glass. "He spent the last five years in Folsom Prison for murder, and somebody murdered him two weeks after his release."

My look asked, *Really?*

I listened intently as Kyra related what she knew of Jeffrey's crime and death.

"Your parents must be devastated."

Kyra nodded. "Mom's been in three-sessions a week therapy ever since. Dad works twelve hour days to avoid Mom and his own thoughts."

"I assume the police investigated Jeffrey's murder."

"They did, but Dad says they've given up."

I sipped wine and thought a moment. I knew two Sacramento Police Department homicide detectives. I met them while I investigated the murders of a busload of 'dead peasants.' The morning I brought the case to its conclusion, while looking down on one of the bad guys, I had telephoned Detective Sergeant 'Harker' Smith to report a fresh corpse. I had not shot the guy who had shot at me, but I knew who had.

I briefly wore an LAPD uniform during my twenties. One graveyard shift I exchanged bullets with a fleeing gang banger. He did not survive, but one of his nine millimeter rounds shattered my hip which got me a medical retirement and enough money to finish law school. That experience and my brief encounters with law enforcement officials since I started investigating for Ed Logan had convinced me cops don't like amateurs.

Cops consider all private investigators except retired cops amateurs. The older badge-toters trying to enhance their monthly pension checks are not considered serious competition because they lack the police department resources they once enjoyed.

So my next words surprised me. I met Kyra's eyes and said, "I know a Sacramento homicide detective. Do you want me to give him a call?"

Kyra smiled.

One might have considered that flash of perfect teeth a female's response to successfully convincing a male to do her bidding.

If you look up 'cynic' in your Funk & Wagnall's you'll see my picture, but I gave Kyra the benefit of my affection for her and assumed she demonstrated her gratitude.

"I don't want you to take away from any active case you have, Dan, but, yes, I would appreciate any information you might obtain. My parents are unhappy Jeffrey's killer has not been caught."

I declined to describe how many murders go unsolved. Kyra's a bright lady and a realist.

4

When Tyler Thompson failed to appear to load his Federal Express truck, his supervisor telephoned Tyler's cell phone number and left a message. Then he called a land line number and left a second message. The third number he had listed next to a name, Gerald Thompson, got him Tyler's father.

Tyler had never missed a scheduled work day, and Gerald, then on duty as a Sacramento Police officer, agreed to check on his son. Gerald radioed his dispatcher, asked for a security check on Tyler, and, at the next parking lot, reversed his patrol vehicle's direction.

The first officer on the scene found Tyler's door unlocked and entered.

Tyler sat motionless on his couch. His head rested on the back, and his open left eye looked up at the ceiling. A broken pool cue protruded from his right eye socket.

5

Sunday morning after my date with Kyra, I found the business card Detective Sergeant Harold "Harker" Smith gave me during a chat near my burning trailer in a Sacramento River RV resort. I telephoned the number and left a message.

Then, instead of going online and reading what I could find of Jeffrey Sanford's conviction and death, I read the Sunday newspaper. I decided a chat with the police sergeant, if I could get one, would help me focus my research.

After the paper and before I would have to pay for another day at my RV resort, I walked Penny to the office and checked out. Then, back at my space, I disconnected my land lines, hooked my trailer to my Jimmy, and drove up, over, and down from Donner Summit to my father's home in Davis, California.

"Even though you would not bet with me the last time I saw you, I'm still willing to buy you breakfast," I said when Harker returned my call the next morning.

"Not necessary, Dan. I got a nice *attaboy* from my chief for solving the bus crash murders which, of course, you, not I, solved. Because I hold the opinion you strongly protect your privacy, you are listed in my report only as a Reliable Confidential Informant.

"Are you calling to report another corpse or exploded travel trailer?"

"You're right about my privacy, Harker, and, no, no corpse this time. My Reno lady friend finally told me last Saturday evening that Jeffrey Sanford was her brother. She said her parents were unhappy the case had not been solved and asked me if I would look into it."

"The Sanford murder is history, Dan," said Harker. "I'm curious why your lady friend waited so long to mention it."

"Her name is Kyra Simmons," I said. "We don't have what most folks would call a 'normal' relationship. We don't see each other often and, when we do, we don't talk about troublesome matters."

"I wish my marriage had been like that," said Harker. "Did Ms. Simmons mention Tyler Thompson?"

"No. Who is Tyler Thompson?"

"Where are you, Dan?"

"At my father's home in Davis."

"I'll meet you at the Black Bear Diner in half an hour."

"In both cases the shooter got close enough to shoot a twenty-two bullet through his victim's right eye," said Harker. "He followed the bullet with a short section of broken pool cue."

We sat in a booth in the far northeast corner of the restaurant. I had a cup of coffee and a plate of diced ham and scrambled eggs and country potatoes in front of me.

Harker confessed he had eaten a McDonald's bacon-egg-and-cheese biscuit during his drive to his office that morning so he just had coffee.

"While I would never admit to leaving any stones unturned in the Sanford investigation, we have dug under the stones and down to the earth's core in the Thompson case because his father is a cop. I expect Lieutenant Steele to call me in sometime soon and chew me out for spending too much time on the case."

"What did you find?" I asked before I forked pink and yellow into my mouth.

"My coroner buddy, Webster Webfoot, Doctor Webster, actually, did the autopsies on Sanford and Thompson. The slug he found in each brain was twenty-two caliber and weighed slightly less than twenty-nine grains."

"Really?" I said. "Aren't most twenty-two rounds forty grains?"

"Some are thirty-six," said Harker. "The twenty-two short is twenty-nine grains."

"The last time I saw one of those I wore a Boy Scout uniform at an indoor firing range. One of our leaders was a pistol shooter and took us shooting even though there's no merit badge for it."

"I couldn't find a store in the greater Sacramento area that sold any twenty-two shorts recently," said Harker. "In fact, most sporting goods stores don't carry them because they cost five times as much as twenty-two long rifle rounds which is what everybody shoots."

"I would like to know why twenty-two rounds have doubled in price in a very short time."

"I asked about that," said Harker. "One guy told me the price of brass, like a lot of other things, has taken a big jump."

"I read somewhere," I said, "that Mafia hit men preferred to use a small revolver loaded with twenty-two shorts for close range assassinations. Some shorts are subsonic, and two rounds in the head are just as deadly as larger bullets in the torso. With a suppressor a twenty-two short makes about the same noise as a mouse fart."

"I've never heard a mouse fart," said Harker.

"You haven't?" I said. I smiled and added, "Neither have I. One of the mafia hit men who turned on and testified against his bosses a few years ago used that description. He also called his pistol a mouse gun"

"Because Sanford's murder was so clean, the idea a Goldman family member had hired a professional hitter rested in my mind until the Thompson murder," said Harker. "Then I looked for a connection between Sanford and Thompson, but I found nothing except both went to the same school, joined the same fraternity, and were pals notwithstanding the fact Thompson testified against Sanford at his preliminary hearing."

"They stayed pals?" I asked then forked another bite of breakfast.

"According to Folsom Prison visitation records, Tyler Thompson was the only Sigma Pi fraternity brother to visit Sanford during his stay there," said Harker. "He saw Sanford about once every three months during the first year then tapered off to once each Christmas season and Sanford's birthday anniversary.

"According to the records guy I talked to there, that's not bad for a non-relative," added the detective.

"It's good to have a pal," I said.

"Webster Webfoot said the initial wound track in the Sanford case suggests the shooter is five seven to five nine. He believes Thompson took his bullet while sitting on his sofa, but, even so, there was a slight upward angle in the wound track between his right eye and the first bounce off the back of his skull."

"So the killer sat on the couch next to Thompson rather than stood in front of him?"

"Probably," said Harker, "and the bullets going into each victim's right eye suggests the shooter is left handed."

I took a bite of sour dough toast.

"There was no forced entry to either residence in either murder," said Harker. "I believe Sanford opened the front door to someone he knew or at least someone he had no reason to fear."

"I can't get the idea of a professional out of my mind yet," I said. "Remember Stone?"

"I meant to call you," said Harker. "We identified him through his fingerprints."

"Who was he?"

"A Brit named Reginald Alexander Hargreaves. Before he went into the assassination business in the United States, he was a non-commissioned officer in the Special Air Service. The colonel I talked to declined to reveal the details, but Hargreaves got involved in some incident that caused him to resign or get his next re-enlistment denied. He evidently found more use for his training in the U S of A than at home. Or more money."

"That military training and attitude supports John Littmann's declaration he did not pay Stone, er, Hargreaves, to kill me by blowing up my trailer while he thought I would be sleeping in it," I said.

"The way that case ended saved the taxpayers a bundle of money and made my chief happy," said Harker as he lifted his coffee cup.

I nodded. "May I assume you checked whether Sanford made any enemies while in Folsom?"

"I did, and he didn't," said Harker. "At least not officially. Not every enemy makes it into the record. More important, though, nobody from Sanford's section of the block got released within a few weeks of his date."

I forked a bite of ham and eggs.

"I didn't work that trail after Thompson's murder, though."

I chewed. "Maybe Sanford and Thompson opened their doors to a hitter dressed as a U P S delivery man or a Jehovah's Witness."

"Could be," said Harker, "but it appears Thompson not only let the shooter inside his apartment, he invited the guy to have a seat next to him on his sofa."

"Maybe the hitter was a sales person who managed to get more than a foot in the door. My dad complains he gets way too many uninvited visits from bible thumpers, politicians, house painters, lawn mowers, and dirt sucker sales persons. Both male and female."

"I considered the possibility somebody had made an appointment to try and sell something," said Harker. "I got both victims' phones and noted all the saved calls. I checked all the callers *and* all the victims' callees. I got nothing."

"It still might have been a cold visitor selling something the victim had an interest in." I sipped coffee.

"I didn't know either victim, of course, but I can't think of a single thing a young man in his late twenties might be willing to invite somebody in to sell to him."

"How about a well-endowed, very mature Girl Scout selling cookies? Doesn't everybody like Thin Mints?"

"Great minds think alike, Dan." Harker smiled back, "but only the little girls come to my door. And they are always in pairs with two wary mothers standing behind them."

"Did you find any evidence Thompson indulged in any controlled substances?" I asked.

"Good question, Dan, and the shooter may have been a weed smoking pal. Thompson had a prescription for medical marijuana because he supposedly suffered from glaucoma. Forensics found a baggie and several smoking devices in his apartment.

"Lieutenant Steele gave me the unpleasant task of advising Thompson's father of his son's habit," added Harker. "The father didn't seem too shocked, but he asked me not to mention anything to Tyler's mother."

"Any evidence Tyler was re-selling from his stash?"

Harker shook his head and sipped coffee. "No, but that doesn't preclude such activity. Forensics found quite an assortment of hairs, fibers, and prints in Thompson's apartment, but, then, it was a *guy's* apartment, and that was to be expected. None of the hairs, fibers, or fingerprints led anywhere."

"I assume you, finest kind detective that you are, have some idea why the killer stuck pieces of broken pool cues in both victims' eyes."

"Yep," said the detective. "I think the shooter is tied in some way to the bar fight during which Sanford used his pool cue to try to knock Joshua Goldman's head over the center field fence. Or at least through the big screen television bolted to the wall behind him.

"It can't literally be a biblical 'eye for an eye' though," said Harker, "because Goldman wasn't blinded."

"Of course not," I said.

"I looked up that old testament verse," added Harker. "Did you know the list goes beyond an eye for an eye? It includes a burn for a burn and a life for a life."

"Except now it's two lives for one," I said.

"That it is," said Harker. "The shooter may have difficulty with math."

I forked a bite of ham and gave the cynical detective a small smile.

"Another thing bothers me," said Harker. "If I was the shooter, I would have picked off the other fraternity brothers *before* Sanford's release from Folsom. That way he would be sweating like a pig when he walked through those prison gates.

"I'm wondering why he waited."

I swallowed. "Pigs don't sweat, but maybe Sanford's release triggered the spree."

"Could be," said Harker.

"The piece of pool stick is an interesting signature."

"Definitely," said Harker as I forked another bite. "I checked the local stores that sell pool tables and supplies, and there has not been a run on cues.

"I also chased down every person I could find who was known to have been in the bar the night Goldman died. I didn't find them all, of course, because most of them scattered when they heard an approaching siren.

"I'm lucky Goldman didn't have a Facebook account with a thousand 'friends,' but I talked with students who knew him and his professors. They all have solid alibis for one murder or the other.

"Some alibis are better than others," added Harker, "but, at this point in time, everybody is covered."

"Did the lovely Detective Mosier help you with that grunt work?"

"Susan got promoted to sergeant and sent back to Vice," said Harker. "She hated Vice before making it to Homicide, but as a sergeant she doesn't have to dress like a whore any more.

"Sacra-tomato, like most cities these days, has money troubles," said Harker. "The city planned to lay off eighty cops, but a federal grant let them keep about thirty. Some older officers are retiring because the job has reached the point where it's no fun anymore. Patrol cops race from one call to another only to be chewed out by some irate citizen complaining they called more than an hour earlier. There's no time for pro-active police work, and now the Supremes have ordered the state to cut the prison population by forty thousand."

"From what I read," I said, "California's recidivism rate is pretty high."

"It sucks big time, Dan. Two-thirds of parolees released to the Sacramento area will be back in prison within two years."

"As I recall, Supreme Court Justice Kennedy wrote the opinion on your overcrowded prisons, and he's a Californian," I said. "I have to assume some lawyer presented that recidivism rate during oral argument before the panel of nine."

"I, too, assume somebody did," said Harker, "but the ruling doesn't mean the Department of Corrections will suddenly open the felony floodgates. They'll drag their feet trying to decide who stays and who gets out. And, before they cut anybody loose, Governor Brown may get his way and send a huge number of prison felons to the county jail from whence they came. Everybody agrees that would satisfy the Supreme Court's ruling."

"Why did you Californians elect Jerry Brown, my dad calls him Moonbeam, again?" I asked. "Didn't anybody in law enforcement point out his liberal appointments to the state Supreme Court during his first term? Didn't anybody remind the voters of that court's screwy rulings and the voters' subsequent removal of three of its members?"

"Several folks pointed out Charlie Manson and Sirhan Sirhan would have been gassed years ago but for Rosey Bird and her pals overturning the death penalty," said Harker. "I guess those same voters didn't like Meg Whitman trying to buy a governorship with a hundred and forty-four million dollars of her own money. Brown may have been the lesser of two evils."

"I would have voted for the stranger," I said.

"Brown won by thirteen points," said Harker.

I nodded. "I watched a two-night later rerun of Bill Maher's Friday night cable show with Lansing last evening. When talking about the Republican candidates already making noise for the twenty twelve presidential election he said anybody could get elected in this 'dumb, fucking country.' His words."

"He was right," said Harker. "Wasn't it Reagan who said only the average and dumber students run for public office and get elected to govern us? Didn't he say the smart students go into business?"

"Something like that." I sipped coffee. "I've been on the road and may have missed it, but I've seen nothing of a serial killer loose in Sacramento."

"Per police procedure, I extracted promises from James and Kimberly Sanford not to mention anything about the bullet that killed their son or the broken pool cue to anyone.

I did the same, probably unnecessarily because Thompson's father is a cop, with those family members.

"So far that information has not appeared in the media."

"That's good," I said.

"Some newspaper reporter found and reported Jeffrey Sanford's no contest plea and prison sentence," added Harker. "One letter to the editor writer in the *Bee* said people don't meet nice people in prison and maybe Sanford made an enemy there."

"His sister, Kyra, doesn't think that," I said. "Have you warned the other bar fighting Sigma Pis they may be targets?"

Harker looked into his cup a moment. "The other fraternity brothers who went Fist City that night no longer reside in my jurisdiction, Dan. However, because they were stand up enough guys to stay at the saloon and talk with the uniforms and me after Goldman hit the floor, I called them after the Thompson murder.

"I did not mention the broken pool cues in the victims' eyes, but I told each of them the two murders might not be a coincidence."

"Did they all graduate from college?"

"Yes."

"Then they should be smart enough to put two and two together."

I took my last bite of ham and egg, chewed a moment, and then pushed the last of my toast into my mouth.

"Hopefully," said Harker, "but we both know anybody can kill almost anybody else in this wonderful country. Not only do we have a big gun selling business here, Mexican officials are complaining we are arming the drug cartels below our border."

After I chewed and pushed my plate a few inches closer to the center of the table, I asked, "Did you talk with Goldman's parents?"

"Joshua had an emergency contact card in his wallet with his mother's info on it. I had to call her and pass the sad news. I also met with her in Webfoot's shop after she trained up from Glendale to make arrangements for Joshua's body to be shipped south. Identifying the body was hard on her.

"I had not yet visited Joshua's residence, so I offered to drive Mrs. Goldman there," said Harker. "After she calmed a bit, she said Joshua's father died from lung cancer within months of Joshua's Bar Mitzvah. She said Joshua was an only child who turned eighteen while still in high school and, as a legal adult, joined the Army without telling her. He left for basic training the Monday after he graduated and did six years active duty which included at least two tours in Iraq. He enrolled at Sac State before he got out.

"I'm sure you asked about close Army buddies who might want to avenge his death," I said.

"Millicent said Joshua's emails never mentioned any fellow soldiers by name. She said Joshua was a very private person who kept to himself. He had a couple of school and temple buddies before his father died, but they faded afterward and his mother didn't know if Joshua stayed in contact with them.

"Mrs. Goldman pulled Joshua's key ring from his personal effects," added Harker, "and we entered his apartment together. We found it spotless which evidently surprised Mrs. Goldman. She turned to me and asked if the police had visited and cleaned it before we arrived."

I chuckled. "Like that would happen."

"Yeah, right," said Harker. "I could see the place was clean, but I assured her we had no reason to make a warrantless entry. After I had first called her with the bad news, I had decided to wait for her arrival and get her permission to enter.

"As we looked around the apartment, we discovered the bathroom towels were clean and fresh smelling, a hamper was empty, and the bed sheets had been washed.

"Mrs. Goldman commented that Joshua had not been such a neat child," said Harker, "and I told her I kept my apartment squared away for quite awhile after I got out of the Army. I suggested maybe Joshua did his laundry and cleaned his apartment the day he died."

"Did you see any evidence of a girlfriend?" I asked.

"Not a thing. The only evidence we had of one, and Millicent said Joshua had never mentioned a girlfriend to her, was the girl who kissed him in the bar before she took off like most of the other patrons.

"There was no female sign in the apartment," added Harker. "No second toothbrush, no photos, no tampons stashed under the bathroom sink, no nothing.

"I questioned the manager who told me he didn't think Joshua had a cleaning service, that he had not been inside the apartment, and that he had not seen Joshua with a steady girlfriend."

Harker finished his coffee and looked at me. "It was the girl in the bar, of course. I'm sure she had a set of Joshua's keys. She drove his Honda there, cleaned the place, washed the sheets and towels, packed up her stuff, and locked the deadbolt when she left."

"You're probably right," I said. I drained my coffee cup and added, "Well, Harker, it's been enlightening. Thanks for meeting with me and filling me in. I guess I will tell the lovely Doctor Simmons her brother's murder has gone cold."

Harker nodded. "As frigid as my ex-wife's heart."

I smiled. "I'm not saying I live the perfect life," I said, "but I am convinced having a dog is better than having a wife."

"You are absolutely right, Dan," said Harker. "For one thing, if a dog runs off and leaves you, it won't take half your stuff."

I smiled. "And you never have to wait on a dog. Penny is ready to go wherever I want to go whenever I want to go there."

Harker nodded. "If a dog smells another dog on you, it won't kick you in the crotch."

I wondered where that came from. "Dogs like to go fishing."

"Dogs don't care if you call them by another dog's name."

"Penny is always happy to see me."

"A dog's parents never visit," said Harker.

"Penny never tells me to stop scratching my balls."

Harker nodded. "She probably wonders why you don't lick them instead."

"I sometimes wonder what she's thinking when she looks at me."

"Dogs agree that you have to raise your voice to get your point across," said Harker.

"Penny never wakes me up at night and asks, 'If I died, would you get another dog?'"

"If a dog has babies, you can put an ad in the paper and sell them."

"Penny's been spayed," I said.

"A dog will let you put a studded collar on her without calling you a pervert," said Harker.

When I couldn't think of another one, I said, "We'd better stop, Harker. You're beginning to give yourself away."

"You're right, Dan. Good luck with the girlfriend."

6

I considered whether I should pay a respectful visit to James Sanford, Jeffrey's father. Though I had known Kyra several years, she had said little of her family and had made no offer to introduce me to them. While looking through a Corona bottle at a small campfire one evening, I had concluded meeting parents fell outside the parameters of our relationship. My father knew I had a female friend with a female autistic child, but I had assured him we would never marry.

I did not tell him Kyra had a Judgment of Legal Separation instead of a Judgment of Dissolution of Marriage from her husband.

Had Jeffrey Sanford's murder not had a sequel, I might have returned to Reno and told Kyra it, like a great percentage of all murders, would likely remain unsolved. However, so I could tell Kyra I had, I decided to learn more about the Sigma Pis and Joshua Goldman.

I took Penny for a walk to the greenbelt two doors down from my father's house then returned to his air conditioned home office. I used his desktop computer to read every *Sacramento Bee* story I could find about the bar fight and criminal prosecution of Jeffrey Sanford.

When I wore the LAPD uniform, the dispatcher occasionally directed me to a saloon to investigate an assault and/or battery. By the time I arrived, I often found a single victim and zero witnesses other than bartenders and waitresses who usually declared they had been busy working and had seen nothing.

That the Sigmas stood together after Sanford struck Goldman with his pool stick surprised me. I wondered if their 'brotherhood' pledges forced this behavior on them or if the bouncers blocked their exit. Most of them were innocent of any criminal activity except fighting in public which is rarely prosecuted by deputy D As who know juries have difficulty placing the blame on one combatant.

After hearing his rights from the uniformed police officer that arrested him, Jeffrey Sanford said he wanted the family lawyer present during questioning. While he was handcuffed and placed in a patrol car, other uniformed officers interviewed bartender Henry Colfax, Tyler Thompson, Curtis Hendricks, Truman Breckinridge, William King, and Michael Thomas. And, after he arrived on the scene, Detective Sergeant Smith re-interviewed Colfax and each young man.

I labeled the opposing group The Laker Boys, but I doubted more than one or two of them knew each other before the night of the brawl. The bartender, Henry Colfax, the key unbiased witness, told the police he did not notice any of them enter the Overtime together. He thought most of them were already present when the Sigmas entered together and filled an area near a corner pool table.

Colfax said all of the Sigmas ordered beers. When they had them, two started talking with unattached women, two others started a pool game, and the remaining pair opened cell phones.

Unlike the 'stand-by-your-brother' Sigmas, The Laker Boys were not interviewed by the cops at the scene because they, like most of the other Overtime patrons, disappeared at the sound of approaching sirens.

The prosecutor relied on Colfax for key testimony at Jeffrey Sanford's preliminary examination in a municipal court room. He estimated that by the time the fight started eight young women sat at several small tables near the three pool tables which had been leveled on a hardwood floor below a large screen television. A female or two cheered either a Sigma or a Laker Boy during the one-on-one pool games. They also cheered either the Kings or the Lakers during the televised game.

Colfax said all but one of the females scattered immediately after Goldman hit the floor. One young woman, a tanned girl with short black hair, hurried to Goldman, knelt next to him, and put her hands on his face. Colfax saw Goldman's lips move, and then the woman nodded, kissed his mouth, and fled.

A waitress working the small tables near the pool tables agreed with Colfax when he said the televised basketball game provided the focal point of the dispute. The employees and the Sigmas agreed the rivalry quickly turned from easy kidding and joking to seriously nasty taunts while Sanford and Goldman played a second game of Nine Ball. Sanford had won the first game with a lucky shot that sunk the nine, and the next in line Laker Boy had agreed Goldman could have his slot for a rematch.

Tyler Thompson told a police officer at the scene and testified at the hearing that the semi-inebriated Goldman teased Sanford with, "You dance around the table like you've got one of your pals' dicks up your ass."

Then, according to Thompson but unconfirmed by Colfax, Goldman moved close to Sanford and said something about Sanford's mother's willingness to sexually entertain Laker fans by the dozen.

Thompson declared that after those words Sanford punched Goldman hard on the face, and then he, Thompson, turned and punched The Laker Boy standing next to him.

Colfax had already told the court how Thompson joined the fray. Colfax said the Laker Boy did not expect the blow, but he punched back at Thompson and may not have seen Goldman drop his cue stick as he grabbed the pool table to stop a fall. After Goldman pulled himself erect, he glared at Sanford, wiped blood from his nose, and then charged the Sigma with a head butt to the abdomen.

After shouting for the bouncers, Colfax said he took his eyes off the action while he reached for a phone and tapped a speed dial number for the police department. He declared he had learned several years earlier not to waste time tapping 9-1-1 and attempting to rapidly explain a bad situation to a listener who would connect him with the police department where he would have to repeat himself.

When he looked back toward the pool table, Colfax testified he saw four separate fights in progress. He said he watched Sanford end his particular battle by swinging his cue at Goldman, striking Goldman's head, and watching the Laker Boy collapse to the floor.

Though the responding uniformed police officers, and Harker when he arrived, questioned many people in the bar, only Thompson supported Colfax's statement with the declaration that, after he stopped fighting with his selected adversary, he saw Sanford standing above Goldman holding his pool cue like a baseball bat.

At the hearing Thompson testified Sanford looked at him after he struck Goldman with his cue. Then Sanford looked back down on his victim, dropped his cue on the floor next to his victim, stepped to a nearby table, lifted his beer bottle, took a drink, and then moved to the bar where he stayed until arrested.

Thompson said he stepped to the bar beside Goldman and waited with him for the cops to arrive.

Thompson duplicated Colfax's description of the dark-haired girl who kissed Goldman, but he did not know her and had never seen her before that night.

During cross-examination by Sanford's attorney, Thompson admitted the District Attorney had charged him with assault and battery and had agreed to drop all charges in exchange for truthful testimony at the preliminary hearing and at trial.

In addition to Colfax and Thompson, a police forensics specialist testified he found a trace of Goldman's blood on the fat end of the cue which also had finger and palm prints from both of Sanford's hands near the center.

An Emergency Medical Technician testified Joshua Goldman was conscious when he first reached him in the Overtime saloon. The patient faded during transit, and his heart stopped before the ambulance reached the hospital.

An emergency room physician testified he found no life signs in Goldman and declared him deceased.

Assistant Coroner Doctor Webster testified he had performed an autopsy on Joshua Goldman. He gave his expert opinion Goldman's death resulted from a massive subdural hematoma.

The judge ruled sufficient evidence had been presented to hold Sanford for a homicide trial in the Superior Court. Immediately following the court's ruling, Goldman, on advice of the criminal defense specialist retained by James Sanford and pursuant to a previously arranged agreement with the District Attorney, asked to be arraigned and pleaded no contest to voluntary manslaughter. He received an eleven year prison sentence. A crowded California prison system and good behavior got him an early parole.

The D A dismissed the charges against Thompson as agreed.

I printed the 'Sanford' newspaper stories then reviewed the few *Bee* articles pertaining to Thompson's murder. As Harker had declared, I found no evidence showing any reporter had tied the two murders together.

I called Ed Logan at his Los Angeles office. Though I occasionally investigate insurance fraud cases for Logan, I do not possess a state issued private investigator's license. I occasionally give people a business card which declares I am a claims specialist for Logan Insurance Services.

As a member of the California and Nevada State Bars, I also carry business cards showing I am a private attorney at law. Those cards show my bar numbers and an email address but no physical address and no telephone number. I do not want to be visited or called. Email communication will have to do until I provide more information which I almost never do.

If a curious person visits either states' bar site, he or she will find my address is a Reno post office box. If that person makes the effort to determine the physical address behind the post office box, he or she will read the Livingston School address

"Thanks for the deposit on the Harwood case, Ed," I said.

"You're welcome, Dan," said Logan. "Have you bought a new motorcycle yet?"

Somebody had burned my dual purpose Suzuki six-fifty at the Sturgis Motorcycle Rally while I searched for "dead" Harwood. I never did learn if some hard core biker thought I should buy American or if the "dead" guy had spotted me on my bike while I searched for him and burned my two-wheeled machine as a communication of discouragement.

"Not yet. I'm involved in another matter and haven't had time to look for one.

"That's why I called, Ed," I added. "I didn't know it until she called me a few days ago and asked for my help, but my lady friend had a younger brother. I say 'had' because the Folsom prison authorities released Jeffrey Sanford after he served five years for voluntary manslaughter. Somebody murdered him in his parents' home twelve days later."

"That must have surprised you," said Logan. "Her having a criminal brother."

"It did. We don't talk much about our families," I said, "I had mentioned meeting a Sacramento police department detective while working the dead peasants case for you, and she asked if I could find out if the police were still working on Sanford's case.

"I drove down the mountain to my dad's house and had a chat with the detective. He said Jeffrey's case went cold fast, but a couple of weeks ago another young man was murdered using the same M O.

"I plan to nose around a bit, and I want your permission to make up a life insurance story and flash a Logan Insurances Services card if necessary."

"Not a problem, Dan," said Logan. "I'll let you know if anybody calls."

"Thanks, Ed. I don't expect great success, so feel free to interrupt me with any new case that causes you indigestion."

"I will. Good luck, Dan."

7

Doug Hobart telephoned Elena Hendricks at the Huntington Beach condominium she shared with her brother, Curtis.

"Is your brugly other coming to work today?"

"He's not there already?"

"Nope."

"I just got up," said Elena. "Let me check his room."

Two minutes later Elena said, "He's not here, and, to tell you the truth, I can't tell if he even came home last night because he doesn't make his bed every morning."

"He wasn't there last night?" asked Hobart.

"Not before I went to bed about eleven, but that's not unusual. He's popular with the ladies, you know."

"I know he *tells* us about some of his conquests, but we don't always believe him. Whatever. I guess we'll make do without him today. Thanks, Elena."

"Not a problem. See ya."

8

Small groups of 'let's get together for a beer after work' customers trickled in to the Overtime sports bar as the little hand moved past the five. Some wore serious office attire, and others dressed casually.

I sat at the bar and drank a bottle of Corona as slowly as possible. The many large screen televisions hanging on the walls showed replays of a soccer match, a boxing match, a basketball game, and a major league baseball game. Two screens on opposite walls had a commentator talking with a man in a NASCAR racing suit.

The female bartender who served me admitted to working only two months and knowing nothing of Joshua Goldman's death. She told me Henry Colfax started his shift at six, and I decided to wait.

Colfax approached me as I neared the end of my Corona.

"Ready for another, sir?" he asked.

About fifty years old, Colfax's lean physique and tanned face reflected time in the sun, regular visits to the gym, and zero consumption of the products he purveyed. His closely cropped hair showed some grey, but I guessed he dyed his dark brown goatee and mustache.

I put a twenty dollar bill on the bar and put my left forefinger on it. "I'm willing to pay twenty dollars for it if I can get a couple of answers with it."

"Depends on the questions," said Colfax.

"According to Detective Smith and the *Sacramento Bee,* you were here the night Jeffrey Sanford killed Joshua Goldman," I said. "I'm trying to figure out which of Goldman's pals may have killed Sanford three months ago right after he got out of Folsom."

"Why?" asked Colfax.

I kept my left finger on the bill and pulled a Logan business card from my shirt pocket with my right hand. I put it next to the twenty and turned it with my right forefinger so Colfax could read. As I did so, I said, "We paid off on the Sanford family's life insurance claim, and, if we can find enough evidence for a wrongful death lawsuit, we might try to get some of it back."

Colfax looked at my card then met my eyes.

"I think you're pissing in the wind, Mister Ballantine. Goldman might or might not have been part of a group of six or seven guys and several young women. I didn't see anything unusual about any of them that might make me think one might be a murderer."

I pushed the bill and the card toward him a few inches, lifted my fingers from them, and pulled my hands back to the edge of the bar. "I don't think Mister Logan really expects me to find anything," I said, "but things are slow and I had another reason to be in this area."

Colfax nodded, put my card in his shirt pocket, took my bill, and said, "I'll get you another Corona, Mister Ballantine."

"Thank you, Mister Colfax," I said. "No lime, please."

I finished my beer then drove slowly and carefully to the California State University at Sacramento. I parked near the Sigma Pi house and let Penny out to pee on the manicured grass.

Inside a young man aimed a finger at a second young man and said, "Talk to Mario. He's our secretary."

Mario Martinelli admitted his secretarial role and read my attorney card. Unconcealed disdain marred his face as he looked up at me and said, "Let's go talk over there."

He cocked his head toward a pole lamp guarding the corner of the room from a safe position between a pair of matching and touching arm chairs.

Mario stopped where the arms met and turned to face me. He did not suggest we sit.

I gave him my 'hard' look and said, "If your time is too valuable to give me a few minutes, Mister Martinelli, I will leave now. I will put a note in my file noting the date, the time of day, and your name. Then, when another former member of this Sigma Pi chapter is found dead with a twenty-two bullet in his skull, I will tell his family I wanted to warn him but you were too busy to give me his phone number."

"What do you mean 'a twenty-two bullet in his skull'?"

"Are you too busy drinking, er, studying to watch the television news or read a newspaper, Mister Martinelli?" I asked. "Jeffrey Sanford and Tyler Thompson, both former Sigmas Pis from this chapter, were found shot to death during the last few months."

"Of course I am aware of those murders," he said. He glanced at my card. "But you are not with the police, and my father, who is also an attorney, has often advised me not to talk to an attorney I do not know about *any single thing.*"

"I may similarly advise my own son when he is older, Mister Martinelli, but I am talking to you as the current secretary of this Sigma Pi chapter and I expect a certain level of courtesy," I said. "You may not invite me to sit while we chat, but, when two of six known Sigma Pi

attendees at a bar fight at the Overtime saloon six years
ago have been murdered, I should think current members,
including the secretary, would be curious and helpful to
anyone working to solve those murders."

Mario frowned slightly. "Please have a seat, Mister
Ballantine."

When we were both seated and looking at each other,
Mario spoke softly, "That bar fight is local legend here.
Jeff Sanford went to prison for killing that guy."

"And he was murdered soon after his release," I said.
"And Tyler Thompson, a Sigma Pi member six years ago,
has also been murdered."

Martinelli paused a moment then met my eyes. "I
didn't know Thompson was a Sigma Pi, and I don't recall
any of the media mentioning it. Nor do I know the names
of other Sigma Pi members who may have been at the bar
the night of the fight."

"Thompson was a Sigma Pi, and the names of the
others involved were listed in newspaper articles six years
ago," I said. "And while it is possible Thompson's murder
is not connected to Sanford's, my client does not believe
in coincidence."

"Do you think somebody murdered them because
they were former Sigma Pi members?"

"Has murdered and may still be murdering," I said.
"But my thoughts are not relevant, Mister Martinelli. My
client wants me to talk with William King, Curtis
Hendricks, Truman Breckinridge, and Michael Thomas.
They were all members of this chapter and present in the
Overtime saloon when Jeffrey Sanford killed Joshua
Goldman. Will you give me their present addresses and
telephone numbers?"

Martinelli read my card again then looked up at me.
"I will give you their addresses, Mister Ballantine, but
Sigma Pi policy prevents me from giving you their
telephone numbers without a subpoena. Additionally, that

policy requires that I communicate with each of those former members and tell him I have given you his address."

"That's not a problem with me," I said. "Feel free to give them my email address, too. It's on the card, and I would be happy to make appointments with them."

I gave Secretary Martinelli a small smile and asked, "Does Sigma Pi publish a directory of members' and former members' addresses?"

Mario nodded. "We publish an annual yearbook for active members. It contains former members' names, their graduation year, and, if they have requested we do so, their company names, addresses, and telephone numbers. Every five years we publish a directory which is made available to members and former members as a P D F attachment to an email. We used to send everybody a hard copy, but that got too expensive. If former members want a hardcopy version, they have to order one and send a donation to cover printing and shipping costs.

"They usually send more, of course."

"Are the current members' photos in the yearbook?"

"Yes," said Mario, "along with relevant biographical information and their home city."

"Are either of these directories available to the public?" I asked.

"For a fee, yes," said Mario.

"So a stranger could have a copy of, say, the yearbook from six years ago or the most recent five year directory?"

"Yes."

"Okay," I said. "If you'll give me the addresses of the four former members I named, I will thank you and be on my way."

The original purchaser of my GMC truck paid for all the latest technical gadgets including a 'hands off' phone connection. Its loud chime filled my cab as I drove away from the Sigma Pi house. I glanced at the screen, saw 'Harker,' and said, "Hello, Sergeant Smith."

"You sound funny, Dan."

"The slightly used truck I bought after Stone blew up my last one lets me talk with both hands on the wheel."

"The cop in me is pleased to hear you are a law abiding driver, Dan," said Harker. "I thought you might be interested in a call I just took from a So Cal homicide dick. The Huntington Beach part of So Cal."

"Why would I be interested?"

"Curtis Hendricks was found dead last night."

"Is that the same Curtis Hendricks who attended our infamous Overtime bar fight six years ago?" I asked.

"Same guy."

"May I assume he had a twenty-two short in his brain and broken pool cue through his right eye?"

"He had a stick in his eye," said Harker, "but I don't have confirmation of the expected bullet yet. They'll let me know the autopsy results sometime soon."

"Was he at home?"

"No. A city employee checking closed beach parking lots found him sitting up behind the wheel of his pickup truck."

9

I planned my drive to Southern California with two goals: I wanted an Original Tommy's chili cheeseburger, and I wanted to avoid stop-and-go Los Angeles traffic. I got stuck one time pulling my fifth-wheel trailer in a morass of motor vehicles, and I will do anything to avoid a repeat of that frustrating activity.

Before I left Lansing's home in Davis, I went online to make sure the Original Tommy's at Beverly and Rampart Boulevards remained open twenty-four hours. I knew I would have difficulty finding a place to park my rig near there, but I could not drive by without a chili cheeseburger. While working graveyard patrol for the LAPD, I averaged three point five per week.

They were better when Tommy's cooks hand-formed thick patties from fresh ground beef, but, in my opinion, they are still worth extra driving miles.

A few years back I bought Lansing a book published by National Geographic for his birthday. Nathaniel Lande compiled *The 10 Best of Everything, An Ultimate Guide for Travelers.*

Lansing smiled as he unwrapped the book. "This looks interesting."

I said, "Don't give it too much weight, Dad. He left Original Tommy's off the hamburger list on pages two twenty and two twenty-one."

Lansing opened the book and glanced at those pages. "You're right, Dan. Not only did he omit Tommy's, he put In-N-Out Burger at number two. He is obviously not as well traveled as he could be."

Original Tommy's website contained a list of his Southern California business sites including one in Fountain Valley that remained open until three a.m. on weekend mornings.

I went to Google Maps and enlarged one to a size which revealed nearby businesses. I noticed the Fountain Valley Original Tommy's sat close to a Sports Authority near the intersection of the freeway and Magnolia Boulevard. I had planned to leave the 405 freeway and travel south on Beach Boulevard to my Huntington Beach RV resort, but I found Magnolia ran parallel to Beach and all the way to the ocean a mile or so east. I predicted the sports business would, at two a.m., have an empty parking lot large enough for my truck and trailer rig.

I ignored the offramp for the original Original Tommy's and continued south into Orange County and left the freeway on the Magnolia Boulevard offramp. When I reached the closed sporting goods store, I parked atop tandem spaces in the empty lot and loosed Penny into the cool night air. I listened to the roar of vehicles passing on the nearby freeway while she sniffed and marked the grassy parkway on Recreation Circle.

The odd hour felt refreshing because I had disrupted our four hundred and thirty mile drive south along Interstate 5 with a three-hour nap near Coalinga. The government built a so-called Rest Area near the Avenal exit, but I have difficulty sleeping in those places. There are too many big rigs rolling by the long spaces where I have to park my rig. And in the warm central valley summer, the truckers sleep with their powerful diesel engines idling and their air conditioners running.

I don't know how they do it nor do I know how the truckers will cope when California's nanny government outlaws such idling as it continues its efforts to 'green' itself. I cannot imagine wearing a California Highway Patrol uniform and being assigned to awaken sleeping truckers to write them a pollution citation.

I had pulled into the Rest Area long enough to study my map. A few miles later I left the freeway where State Route 33 heads west to Coalinga. I turned right on Calaveras Avenue and pulled into the Coalinga Airport parking lot as darkness settled on the valley. I have learned that small airports are usually quiet during the night time hours, and nobody questions an unfamiliar vehicle.

After her walk and sniff, I put Penny in my truck, hurried to the Original Tommy's branch store, and enjoyed a chili cheeseburger, hot fries, and a large cola in the almost empty restaurant.

Three hours later a knock on my trailer door and Penny's single bark awakened me from my second nap of the night. After my meal, I had driven a few miles to the RV resort across the Pacific Coast Highway from the beach in Huntington Beach and parked in the registration lane.

I rolled from my bed, slipped into a pair of moccasins, told Penny to stay, stepped to my door, and opened it.

"Are you Mister Ballantine?" asked a middle-aged woman.

"Yes, ma'am."

"C'mon in, and I'll get you registered," she said. "Then you can move your rig to your assigned spot and hook up."

At two fifty that afternoon I sat on a hard bench under the curious eyes of a cute, lightly freckled, twenty-something receptionist in a waiting room at Beach Headquarters on Pacific Coast Highway. I'm sure she thought I was overdressed in jeans, a long-sleeve shirt, and hiking boots, but I don't feel comfortable interviewing people in shorts and sandals even if I'm in the self-proclaimed Surf City, USA.

I had called a few minutes after eight a.m. and learned Bradley Bowen, the employee who found Curtis Hendricks' corpse, was expected to start his swing shift at three p.m. that afternoon.

Bowen approached me, and I decided the Beach Director could have hired him on appearance alone. A lean, tanned, nearly hairless man of about twenty-five, the sun had bleached his short, light brown hair several shades lighter than natural, and paddling a surf board through salt water waves had broadened his shoulders. He wore the standard beach uniform of board shorts and a flowery short-sleeved shirt which he had left unbuttoned. His strapped sandals appeared to be a few dollars up from the tire-soled, Mexican-made *huaraches* the Beach Boys sing about.

I handed him an insurance card and suggested we step outside so the receptionist could focus on the wall instead of two handsome men.

We stepped to the east end of the building and stood in the shade. I could see the ocean, and I smelled salt water on the light breeze.

"What can I do for you, Mister Ballantine?" asked Bowen.

"My company is administering Curtis Hendricks' life insurance policy," I lied. "I read the newspaper article, but I'd like to know if there's anything you might want to add to what you told the media people."

"Not really," said Bowen. "The parking lot between First Street and Beach Boulevard closes at ten p.m. I drove through about ten thirty and saw a dark green double-cab Tacoma pickup parked there. It was the only vehicle in the lot. I pulled up behind it, shined a light on the back window, and saw the top of a guy's head over the driver's side headrest.

"I pulled my mike and told him through the loudspeaker it was past time to leave the lot. He didn't move, so I pulled into the empty space next to the right side of the Tacoma. When I looked through the window, I could see something sticking out of the guy's face."

"Out of his eye?"

"Well," said Bowen, "I couldn't tell that until I put a light on him. Then I froze for a second.

"I got out of my unit, stepped around the truck, found the driver's door unlocked, and opened it. When the interior light hit him, I felt my stomach flip. He had the piece of stick in his right eye and dried blood on his face.

"It was gruesome, dude," said Bowen. "I'll never get that picture out of my brain."

I nodded. "What did you do then?"

"I hurried back to my unit and called the police dispatcher. I told her I had found a dead guy and asked her to send a patrol unit to my position."

"Had you patrolled that lot earlier in the evening?"

"Yeah. About eight. There was still some daylight then, and there were still quite a few vehicles in that lot. I don't remember seeing the Tacoma, though."

"Did you wait for the police unit to arrive?"

"Yes. The dispatcher told me not to touch anything and asked me to turn on my emergency flashers on which I did. The first patrol car arrived in about five minutes."

"The newspaper said a bottle of tequila was found in the Tacoma," I said.

"Actually, it was a bottle of pre-mixed margaritas," said Bowen. "It was on the floor in front of the passenger seat. I saw the cop, uh, the officer, put on a glove before he picked it up."

"And a follow up news article said it had been wiped clean of fingerprints," I said.

"That's what I heard," said Bowen. "Somebody said the whole inside of the truck had been wiped clean."

"So my company can rule out suicide," I said.

"Truly, dude," said Bowen, "that was no suicide. No friggin' way."

I smiled. "Did you see anybody walking away from the Tacoma as you entered the lot?"

"No. The cops asked me that, and I told them the same thing. It was a warm summer night, and there was a small group of people walking across the east end of the lot toward the highway. I remember seeing several kids, and the adults carried folding chairs and small ice chests. But I didn't see anybody walking near the Tacoma."

I looked at the Pacific Ocean while I searched for another question.

Bowen looked toward the horizon. "Except for finding bodies, which has only happened once, I love working here. The cool ocean. The warm sand. The laughing children and mostly happy people."

"I can understand that," I said.

"Do you come to the beach often, Mister Ballantine?"

"When I was at U C L A I used to go to the beach once in awhile," I said. "Then I started dating a girl who screamed the same way whether she was being eaten alive by a great white shark or being touched on an underwater leg by a piece of loose seaweed."

Bowen chuckled.

"Thanks for your time, Mister Bowen," I said. "If you think of anything else, please give me a call."

"How much insurance did the dude have?"

"Just enough for a plain casket, a small funeral, and a family wake if they don't eat more than nuts, nachos, and canned beer," I lied.

Bowen smiled. "Nobody needs more than that."

"Still need a hole in the ground," I said.

"They can bury him at sea like the Seals did with Bin Laden," said Bowen. "That's cheap enough."

"Works for me," I said. "Have a good one."

I stepped to my truck and drove to the address Mario Martinelli had given me for Curtis Hendricks. The condo made one end of an older four-unit complex about half a mile inland from the shore. I felt a light breeze from the Pacific and decided the occupants could probably get by without home air conditioning.

When I rang the bell, a petite, dark-haired young woman opened the door. Her puffy eyes and the handkerchief in her right hand told me her mood.

I handed her an attorney card.

She read it and looked up at me.

"Curtis Hendricks is the third former Sigma Pi to be murdered in the past few months," I said. "I drove down here from Sacramento to tell him about the first two."

"If you intended to warn him, you didn't make it in time, Mister Ballantine."

"I know, and I'm sorry for your loss. Have you got time for a couple of questions?"

"Why not?" she said. "Come in."

She turned and left the door open for me.

I entered the neater than I expected living area and, when she pointed, sat in an arm chair.

She remained standing but lifted a glass of dark red liquid from a low table in front of a sofa. She took a drink and looked at me. "I'm Elena Hendricks. Curtis was my brother. My only brother. I'm drowning my sorrows. Want a glass of wine or a beer?"

I had ten years on her, but I wanted to appear sympathetic. I wondered what Miss Manners would recommend in such a circumstance. After a quick think I decided Curtis wasn't *my* brother, *I* wasn't in mourning, and, most important, a beer sounded good.

"A cold beer sounds good," I said.

Elena brought me a long-necked bottle of non-diet Bud then sat on the sofa.

I twisted the cap off, enjoyed a few swallows, and sat in a chair across a low table from her.

"The cops who were here this morning making sure I didn't murder my brother didn't say anything about murdered Sigmas," said Elena.

"They probably didn't know about them," I said. "The first two were murdered several weeks apart in Sacramento. I've got a pal in the Sacramento Police Department. Somebody in the Huntington Beach Police Department noticed a similarity in your brother's murder and the two up north. That person had a conversation with my pal who passed the word to me because he knows I'm working for the family of the first victim."

"What similarity?"

"A bullet through the right eye and the famous Overtime bar fight," I said.

"Overtime bar fight?"

"Your brother and some other members of the Sigma Pi fraternity were involved in a small bar brawl in Sacramento about six years ago. Overtime was the name of the sports saloon where it happened.

"During four or five one-on-one fist fights in progress, a Sigma Pi named Jeff Sanford struck a young man named Joshua Goldman in the head with his pool cue. Goldman collapsed and died before they could get him to a hospital. Sanford went to prison pursuant to a plea bargain. He did five and a half years then somebody murdered him soon after his release early this summer."

"So you and the cops think somebody is killing the Sigma Pis who were involved in that bar brawl?"

I nodded and took a glug of Bud. "Did Curt mention meeting any new people recently?"

Elena shook her head. "No."

"Do you know where he was the night he was murdered?"

"No. He often stops at a sports bar a few blocks from here after work. Used to stop. Callahan's. It's close enough he could walk home if he was too drunk to drive. I sometimes took him back to his car the next morning on my way to class."

"What sort of work did Curtis do?"

"Layed floors. Sometimes carpet, but mostly tile and wood," said Elena. "It took him six years to get a history degree from Sac State, but the only job he could find after he came back home was laying floors for an old high school buddy who never went to college."

"So this area is home, and Curtis went north to school?" I asked.

Elena nodded and took a swallow of beer. "Our dad had the bad luck to get killed in Operation Desert Storm. Curtis was almost three, and Mom was pregnant with me. After dad came home in a box, Mom moved back in with her parents in the older part of Huntington Beach so my grandparents could take care of Curt and me while Mom attended Golden West Community College. After she got an A A degree, she got a job in an insurance company. We stayed with my grandparents until I started first grade then Mom moved us into an apartment.

Mom married Robert, we've always called him Bob, when Curtis was fifteen and I was twelve. Curt wasn't happy about that, and he kept a cold war going with Bob all through high school. I think they mutually agreed it would be better if Curtis went away to school."

"But he came back," I said.

"Yeah, and Bob and Curt got along better after Curt had time to grow up." Elena looked around the living room. "Bob is a good husband to my Mom and good to me and Curt, too. He had this condo when he married Mom, but he decided to buy a house for his new ready-made family. He wanted a yard and a neighborhood with other kids. He kept this condo as a rental property until Curt came back from school, and then he offered to let Curt and me live here for just enough monthly rent to cover the taxes and utilities."

I drank beer. "That's generous."

"I wonder if he'll want it back now that Curt's dead," said Elena. She looked above my head at a picture of a bald eagle flying near a vertical rocky face in nasty weather a few moments then lowered eyes to look at me. "Bob and Mom moved to a condo they bought on Maui about a year ago. They're supposedly on their way here now to help me deal with Curt's funeral."

"Did Curtis ever mention the Sigma bar fight?"

Elena nodded affirmatively. "I'd forgotten about it until you reminded me, but he told me one night while I was still in high school and living at home. Mom and Bob had gone to a movie, and Curt opened a bottle of wine and poured me a small glass. As I recall, Curt was home for the Christmas break. I think he was in his third year at Sac State, and I was in my junior year of high school.

"Curt said he'd been subpoenaed to testify at a court hearing, but the guy who'd hit the other guy took a plea deal before Curt got called to the witness stand."

"So the case was over when Curt told you about it?"

"Yeah," said Elena. "I got the feeling it had happened several months earlier."

"What about when Jeff Sanford was murdered three months ago?" I asked. "Did Curt say anything about it to you?"

"No, but if I had my guess, Curt didn't know about it. He wasn't exactly a six o'clock news kind of guy, and he didn't read newspapers, either."

I nodded and drank beer. I recently read an article that predicts evening newspapers will soon go the way of buggy whips and home milk delivery. Too many people get their news bites on their computers or phones, and, perhaps more important, most young people are apathetic when it comes to current events. They don't vote much, either, which means baby boomers my father's age are now driving the political ship.

"So why did you want to talk to Curt?" asked Elena.

Ah, I thought, *time to tell small lies.*

"Jeffrey Sanford's parents are disappointed with the police department's efforts to find his killer. I know a couple of cops, and the Sanfords hired me to do what I could to prod them to keep the case alive.

"A few days after they retained me, Tyler Thompson was murdered. When I suggested to the Sanford family I chat with the other Sigma Pis present during the bar fight, they agreed."

"Did you plan to warn Curtis that somebody may want to murder him?" asked Elena.

"Well, I would have told him Jeff Sanford and Tyler Thompson were murdered in a similar manner and maybe by the same person," I said. "Now that it appears Curtis has also died the same way, I will include a warning as I talk to the other three former Sigma Pis who were present at the bar fight."

"Are they in Orange County?"

"No. I'm towing my travel trailer, and I will head to Las Vegas from here. Then it's the Oregon coast and Tacoma, Washington state."

"Who's in Vegas?"

"Truman Breckinridge. Did Curtis ever mention him?"

Elena finished her wine and placed the glass on the table. "Not that I recall. He mentioned his time in Sacramento now and then, and he said he had lived in a fraternity house most of the time. He would occasionally tell me a funny story about the stuff they did, but that name doesn't sound familiar.

"Neither did the name of a guy that left Curt a phone message yesterday," said Elena. "I listened to it when I got home from class, and I left it on the phone for Curt.

"He said his name was Mario something, I don't remember, and he worked for the Sigma Pi fraternity. He mentioned your name, said you were an attorney, and told Curt he might hear from you. He didn't say you would visit in person."

"Mario Martinelli?"

"Yeah. That's it."

"Mario is the current Sigma Pi secretary, Sacramento State division," I said. "He didn't want to release information pertaining to former members, but I finally convinced him to give me the addresses of the bar fighters. He said he would notify the former Sigma Pis he had done so.

"It's harder for an attorney to get phone numbers than it used to be," I said. "I would have called to make an appointment with Curt if I had had his number. My call would have included as much of a warning as I could make over the air. Maybe Curt would have come home after work instead of having a beer with his buddies."

"I doubt it," said Elena. "Curt was the type of guy who believed he could take care of himself."

"It's hard to take care of oneself against a man with a gun who wants to kill you," I said.

"True," she said.

When I couldn't think of anything I could say to improve Elena's mood, I finished my beer, placed the bottle on the low table, and got to my feet. "Thanks for the beer and your time. And, again, I'm sorry for your loss."

"Sure." She stood and started toward the door.

"Would you call me if anything develops in your brother's case?"

"Sure." Elena opened the door, and I stepped into the door way. I turned and said, "Thanks, again."

Elena nodded.

Callahan's contained a profitable number of people when I arrived. A few sat at the bar, but most sat in small groups and watched one of six large screen televisions. As I stepped to the bar, I noticed two different baseball games in addition to basketball, soccer, and hockey competitions, and what appeared to be a nine-ball pool tournament on the various screens.

I sat in the center of the bar and placed an insurance card and a twenty dollar bill next to it.

"Sorry," said the bartender as he stopped in front of me. "You just missed happy hour."

I looked around and saw most of the customers had full drinks in front of them.

"That's okay," I said. "I'll have a Corona. No lime."

He fetched my beer and, when he looked down at my bill, noticed my card.

"Did you know Curtis Hendricks?" I asked.

"Yeah. He stopped in a few times a week. Usually with his work buddies."

"Did he stop in here the night he was killed?"

"No, but one of the regulars said they saw him in the parking lot."

"Who was the regular?"

"A guy everybody calls 'Paintman.'" The bartender looked over my left shoulder. "That's him there watching the Angels' game with his pal. He's the guy in the splattered white tee shirt."

I looked behind me. "I see two guys in splattered white tee shirts."

"They're both painters, but the guy called 'Paintman' shaves his chin."

I nodded and slid my twenty toward the bartender. "Keep the change."

He nodded. "Thanks."

I took my bottle and stepped to a small table where two guys in matching paint-spattered outfits, well, the spots did not match, sat looking up at a large-screen television. Bud bottles stood at attention in front of them.

"Good evening, gentlemen," I said.

They both shifted their gaze to me.

I put an insurance card on the table so the 'no-goatee' painter could read it and asked, "Mind if I sit a minute?"

Hairy Paintman looked down and read my card.

"Not a problem," said Paintman, "but I don't need any insurance."

"Me, neither," said Hairy Paintman after viewing the card.

"I'm not selling," I said. "I'm just trying to make sure Curtis Hendricks didn't commit suicide. The bartender said he thought you guys knew him."

The two men looked at each other with the unspoken question, *Do we have time for this guy?*

I saw Hairy Paintman's small nod.

I pulled back a chair and sat.

Paintman looked at me and said, "Yeah, we knew him. But who shoots himself in the eye?"

I smiled. "A bullet in the brain is a bullet in the brain. It doesn't really matter how it gets there, does it?"

"No, I guess not," said Paintman.

"Maybe Curt didn't want blood on the side of his face like a bullet in the temple would leave," I said. "You might be surprised how many people kill themselves in bathtubs and back yards so their family won't have to clean a bloody mess."

"I get it," said Paintman, "but I don't think Curt was the suicide type."

"The 'surprise' statistics say it's hard to tell with some people," I said. "I understand you saw him talking to somebody the evening he died."

"Yeah," said Paintman, "in the parking lot outside."

"You buy us a round?" asked Paintman's pal.

Paintman and I looked at his pal.

"You're interrupting the game of the century, Mister," Hairy Paintman looked at my card again, "Ballantine. That's got to be worth something."

I glanced from one painter's face to the other and then at their bottles which were more than half full.

"Not a problem," I said with a friendly smile. I caught the waitress' eyes, pointed at the two Bud bottles on the table, and said, "Another round here, please."

"How are you doing?" she asked.

I lifted my almost full Corona bottle so she could see it. "Not yet."

She nodded. "Two Buds coming."

"Thanks, man," said Hairy Paintman.

"Yeah," said Paintman. "Thanks."

I nodded and looked at Paintman. "Where was he in the parking lot?"

"Talking to somebody in a minivan," said Paintman.

"Could you see who?" I asked.

"No," said Paintman. "I couldn't see inside the minivan because all the side and back windows were tinted real dark."

"Did you say anything to Curt?"

"Nope."

"Do you recall anything at all about the driver?" I asked. "White guy? Black guy? Short hair? Long hair?"

"Nope. I couldn't even tell you for sure it was a guy. Could've been a soccer mom."

"Probably was a soccer mom," said Hairy Paintman. "Curt was always hitting on the female of the species, and he didn't care whether she was married, single, a mom, or a virgin as long as she had tits and an ass."

Paintman looked at his pal. "He was always getting shit on by all kinds, too."

Hairy Paintman smiled. "You got that right." He looked at me and added, "Ask Bonnie when she brings our beers. I'll bet Curt asked her out a hundred times."

"More like a thousand," said Paintman with a grin. "He even came in wearing a suit and tie one time and asked her out."

Hairy Paintman nodded. "He took the choker off when she said, 'No, Curt, I'm way too high maintenance for you.'"

Both men chuckled and lifted their bottles.

"Nice of her to warn him," I said.

Bonnie placed a new pair of bottles on the table.

I paid her enough for a generous a tip which I hoped would help her maintain herself.

"Thanks again, dude," said Hairy Paintman.

"What he said," said Paintman.

"You're welcome."

We all drank. When our bottles hit the table, I asked, "Do either of you know if Curt had any enemies?"

The painters looked at each other then at me. "Nope," said Paintman. "He came on pretty strong with a girl now and then, but he always backed off when she made it clear she wasn't interested."

"Or he knew he couldn't maintain her," said Hairy Paintman with a smile.

"I saw him get in an argument over a football game with some dude one time," said Paintman. "The dude shut

Curt up by offering to bet a hundred bucks on whatever they were arguing about."

Hairy Paintman grinned again. "That stopped the argument cold. Curt couldn't afford to lose. I heard him complain more than once about his student loan debt."

"I heard that, too," said Paintman.

"His money problems weren't so bad he might want to end it all?" I asked.

"Nah," said Paintman, "he always had beer money."

I took another long pull from my bottle and got to my feet. "Thank you, gentlemen, for your time. Enjoy the beers and the game."

I caught up with Doug Hobart, Curtis Hendricks' boss, a few minutes after eight the next morning. He and his work crew were preparing to pull up old carpet from a small insurance office on Beach Boulevard.

Hobart took three seconds to read my card then gave me twelve more seconds which included one 'no' and one 'I don't have time to talk' before returning to his work.

10

After my non-conversation with Hobart, I let Penny sniff and pee on the thin strip of grass outside the insurance office. Then we returned to the beachside RV resort where I left her in the air conditioned cab with the diesel idling, disconnected my land lines, hooked my trailer, drove to the office, checked out, and entered 'Glendale' into Jimmy's navigation system.

I do not yet trust the tiny woman with the faint British accent that resides inside my dash, and I had planned my route using my California road map the previous evening. Although it was the wrong direction, I knew to head southeast on Pacific Coast Highway about five miles to Newport Beach and turn north on the main boulevard. After a few traffic control lights in a busy business district, the thoroughfare became a northbound freeway.

Considering how many millions of people occupy the Southern California basin and drive solo in their personal vehicles to and from their employment each day, I felt lucky to pull my trailer nonstop on various freeways all the way to Glendale. I slowed to a trotting pace for commuter traffic in several places, but I never came to a complete stop.

Millicent Goldman's home occupied a middle lot in an older neighborhood on Hawthorne Street. The Colorado Street Freeway off the Golden State Freeway got me close to a Home Depot where I parked my rig with hopes nobody would tow it while I visited Joshua Goldman's mother.

Once upon a time I parked my truck in Sparks' Victorian Square parking garage and left Penny inside for fifteen or twenty minutes. When I returned I found an official looking notice taped to my driver's side window just above the door handle. Some do-gooder warned me of the dangers of leaving a dog in a hot vehicle and printed part of a municipal code section which made such act a crime.

I had walked back into the sunlight and read "86" on a nearby bank thermometer. Back in the deep shade of the parking structure I guessed the temperature was ten degrees lower.

My first thought was to buy a thermometer somewhere, verify my estimate, and write the do-gooder a nasty letter advising him my dog, and every dog I had ever known or read about, would have no trouble surviving seventy-six degrees all day long with a bowl of water nearby.

But Victorian Square has no thermometer stores, and I decided driving to one and back to the parking garage was more trouble than I was willing to expend. However, ever since that day, I think about the temperature when I leave Penny in my truck.

Jimmy's thermometer declared the outside temperature had hit ninety-three degrees, and I expected it to climb another two or three while I visited Millicent Goldman. So I leashed Penny and walked her with me the three blocks to the Goldman home. I tied her to a large shade tree in the front yard, told her to sit, stepped to the porch, and rang the bell.

Sixty-something Millicent opened her door and asked, "Mister Ballantine?"

"Yes, Mrs. Goldman. How are you today?"

She smiled and said, "I'm fine, thank you." Then she looked beyond me and asked, "Is that your dog tied to my sycamore?"

"Yes, Ma'am. That's my Penny. I had to park my truck several blocks away in the bright sun and did not want to leave her."

"I like dogs, Mister Ballantine. You may bring her in with you."

"Thank you," I said. "And Penny thanks you, too."

I stepped off the porch, untied Penny, kept her on her leash, and stepped past Millicent into a living room containing well-used maple furniture. A sofa and two matching chairs had maple wings, and a coffee table had raised ends with small, flat storage areas. Two-inch maple fences between the storage boxes made me think the table would work well on a sea going vessel as nothing would slide off it.

"Please have a seat, Mister Ballantine," said Millicent as she pointed at one end of the sofa. "May I provide you with a glass of iced tea?"

I felt certain Millicent would not call me 'Dan' if I asked her to. "That would be nice, thank you. And thank you for seeing me today."

"You are quite welcome."

Penny looked around as if she would like to explore, but, as Millicent left the room, I ordered her to sit near my feet. She did and assumed her regal, out-stretched legs and perked-up ears position.

Millicent soon returned with a tray containing two large glasses of iced tea in tall Waterford crystal glasses in a pattern similar to my father's. I spotted a matching crystal plate containing cookies on the tray between the glasses as she placed it on the table.

Millicent lifted a glass and handed it to me. She took the other one and eased herself into a chair across the table. She took a sip of tea and lowered her glass to her lap. "You said on the phone, Mister Ballantine, that you have questions about Joshua."

"Yes, Mrs. Goldman," I said, "and I want to preface my questions by saying I am sorry for your loss. I do not intend that my visit bring you any additional grief over the loss of your son."

"I lost my husband first and then, a decade later, my son, Mister Ballantine. With the passage of time, God has kindly removed most of my grief. We must all take life as it is given to us, and I found nothing to be gained after Robert died by wallowing in sorrow. That made living with Joshua's passing easier, I'm sure.

"May I ask, before you pose your questions, why you have an interest in Joshua?"

I briefly explained Jeffrey Sanford's murder and lied that I had been retained by his parents to do what I could to assist the police, specifically Homicide Detective Harold Smith, in finding Sanford's murderer. I then mentioned the Thompson and Hendricks murders.

"I see, Mister Ballantine, and I think those are terrible things you have involved yourself in," said Millicent. "Do you think some person Joshua knew is committing these murders?"

Smart lady, I thought. "Do you recall talking with Sacramento Police Detective Harold Smith some years ago?"

"I do. He was the unfortunate officer assigned to call me to tell me of Joshua's death," said Millicent. "I recall his words shocked me, and our first conversation was quite brief.

"I traveled to Sacramento and met him two days later," added Millicent, "and I'm sure our later exchange was more useful to him."

"Detective Smith said you told him Joshua never mentioned any Army buddies in his communications with you," I said. "That seems unusual to me."

Millicent nodded, sipped tea, and then lowered her glass to her lap. "May I give you some background information about my son, Mister Ballantine?"

"Certainly." I took a cookie then leaned back and bit off a small hunk. It was homemade oatmeal raisin still warm from the oven and most excellent.

"Joshua's father, my husband, Robert, was a bank executive and rather more concerned about his work than about being a father. Joshua was our only child, and, as a stay-at-home mom, I involved him in scouting and Little League and as many temple activities as he would permit. We did attend temple as a family when Joshua was a child, and Robert insisted Joshua prepare thoroughly for his Bar Mitzvah.

"It was a few months before that event when a routine physical examination revealed small tumors in both Robert's lungs. He had never smoked cigarettes, but not every lung cancer victim is a smoker."

I nodded and took another bite of cookie.

"Seven months after Joshua's Bar Mitzvah, we checked Robert into Mount Sinai Hospital where he died two weeks later.

"Joshua withdrew into a world of computer video games after we buried his father. He lost all interest in scouting, sports, and temple activities. He stopped being a friend and making friends. His grades dropped from As to mostly Cs."

I sipped sweet iced tea and listened.

"The only bright spot in his life during that time was his dog." Millicent looked at Penny as she continued. "Rabbi Rosen suggested I get Joshua a puppy after my husband died. He thought caring for a dog would draw Joshua back into the real world."

I nodded my agreement and took my last bite of cookie.

Millicent looked up at me. "I bought a male boxer puppy from a temple member who bred them. Joshua named him Ben and took complete care of him. He taught Ben to sit and come and stay. I'm sure he said many more words to

Ben than he did to me during the ensuing years. I would often look into Joshua's room and see him glued to a video screen with Ben sleeping on the floor beside his chair.

"Sometimes Ben would raise his head and look at me," added Millicent. "I could almost hear him asking, 'What do you want?'

"Joshua loved Ben more than anything." She paused and added, "More than me."

Millicent looked down at Penny again, and a smile formed on her face.

"I read many cases as a law student," I said. "We studied all the important U S Supreme Court decisions, of course, but the most memorable, for me anyway, was a one hundred dollar appellate case involving a dog. In a few paragraphs published in the summer of eighteen seventy-two, the Missouri Supreme Court explained why dogs are important to us."

I looked at Millicent to see if she had any interest.

She met my eyes. "Please tell me about it, Mister Ballantine. Ben meant everything to Joshua, and I never completely understood why."

"A farmer who had lost some sheep to dogs and wolves shot a dog on his property. The evidence showed he picked up the dead dog, transported it across the back of his horse, and placed it off his property.

"The dog owner, a neighboring farmer, found the dog and noticed the horse hair on it. He was familiar with the horse, and he sued the shooter for fifty dollars which was the limit in the local court. A man named George Vest who would later get elected to the U S Senate gave a unique and important closing argument to the jury. He never mentioned the dog or its owner, but legal analysts believe his statement swayed the state supreme court when the shooter appealed the case.

"Vest said that a man's best friend could turn on him. A man's children could grow up to be ungrateful no matter how much he loved them or how well he cared for them. A man could lose his money. He could have his good reputation wrongfully smeared.

"But no matter what a man may suffer in life, his dog will never desert him.

"I can't quote Vest's statement verbatim," I said, "but I remember he told the jury a dog will sleep outside in a blizzard if he can be at his master's side. A dog will lick his master's hand even if the man has no food for him. A dog will guard a pauper master as if he were a prince. Vest said that when death takes the master, his dog will be at the graveside, faithful and true."

Millicent smiled. "That was Ben." She looked down at Penny and added, "And Penny, too, I'll bet." She looked up at me.

I nodded. "Supposedly the jury asked the judge if they could award more than the fifty dollar limit. With the judge's permission, the jury awarded the victim farmer one hundred dollars which resulted in the appeal."

I smiled. "I remember our professor commenting that the victim farmer must have really loved that dog. Most men would have bought a new puppy instead of spending more money than the case was worth hiring an attorney and bringing a lawsuit."

Millicent nodded.

I looked around but saw no dog sign in Millicent's living room. "Is Ben here?"

"Ben got cancer at a young age which we learned is not uncommon in boxers," said Millicent. "Joshua felt several small lumps in the loose skin above Ben's chest one day, and we took Ben to a vet."

Millicent frowned at the memory. "I didn't have a lot of spare money at the time. I had been putting what little spare money I had into a special account for Joshua's college expenses. I had always hoped he would attend U

C L A, and I wanted him to live in a dormitory there so he would get a full college experience.

"But Joshua insisted I spend that money on Ben. He said he would attend Pasadena City College and live at home if we could give Ben another year or two."

Millicent looked down at Penny then met my eyes. "I spent three thousand dollars on Ben for surgeries, radiation therapy, and chemo therapy. I know Joshua was grateful, but Ben died shortly after Joshua's eighteenth birthday the following January."

"I'm sorry to hear that," I said. "I lost my mother as a toddler, and my father eased my sorrow with a mutt named Roxie. She finally died of old age during my second year of college. I got Penny at the pound after I finished law school."

Penny looked up at me, and I reached down and scratched her neck.

Millicent looked down at Penny again and studied her. Without looking up she said, "I'm sure Penny is your best friend."

"That she is," I said. "She happily goes where I go whenever I want to go. One time she barked a warning that saved my life."

Millicent looked up at me. "I did not know it until later, but shortly after Ben died, Joshua enlisted in the Army without telling me.

"I should have concluded he had an alternate plan for his life when he refused to let me help him apply to college. He told me it was easy to get into City College, and he would take care of it. But he knew when he said those words he would leave for Army basic training the Monday after his high school graduation."

Millicent blinked rapidly three times and sipped tea while she regained control of her words.

"It was not until the Sunday after his graduation ceremony, over lunch after temple, that he confessed his scheme. He grinned at me and said he wanted to break down doors and shoot people in the face."

I frowned. "I'm sure those were difficult words for you to hear."

Millicent nodded. "Some people say those violent video games don't make the young boys who play them violent, but I disagree.

"Joshua did six years active duty during which he served his first year after his training in Germany. He later told me that was the contract he had made with the recruitment sergeant. Then he went to Iraq where he was quickly promoted to sergeant. After that first year there, he volunteered to go back to Iraq.

"I believe it took most of that time for Joshua to mature past the breaking doors and shooting people stage and realize there is more to life than hurting people or doing what other people tell you to do.

"In any event and for a reason he never mentioned to me, Joshua decided against extending his Army career. He told me, via email, he had been accepted to the California State University at Sacramento."

"I've read that some of today's soldiers use their cell phones and computers to chat with the folks back home every day."

"Joshua did not do that, Mister Ballantine," said Millicent with a note of sadness in her voice. "He only responded with the briefest of notes to the many letters I wrote to him while he was in basic training.

"I discussed the matter with Rabbi Rosen, and he sent a temple elder to visit me here. The elder examined Joshua's desktop computer, told me it was outdated, then helped me choose a new one which he set up for me. He taught me how to use the internet and helped me secure an email address.

"He told me which laptop to buy and send to Joshua," added Millicent. "I did that and shipped it to Joshua when he sent me the address of his second training base. It was only then that Joshua communicated with me, but his emails came no more than once a week."

Millicent smiled again. "I thanked God for those."

"I'm sure you did," I said.

"I often asked Joshua if he was attending Jewish services and if he had met any Jewish soldiers. He never answered those questions. He sent me brief emails from Germany, and, later, Iraq, but he never mentioned any colleagues by name.

"Joshua visited me briefly after he returned to the states from Germany and again after he completed his first year in Iraq. During that visit he told me he had already volunteered to go to back to Iraq for a second tour of duty," added Millicent. "After he arrived there, he emailed me he was in Mosul and was patrolling the city in something he called a Stryker vehicle."

11–Mosul, Iraq, Spring, 2004

Sergeant Joshua Goldman led the recently arrived medical specialist to a large military vehicle.

"Listen up, P F C Alphabet," said Goldman. "I expect every soldier in my crew to know what I am about to tell you. There will, repeat, will be a quiz. How well you do will, repeat, will be a factor on how soon you make Specialist Fourth Class."

"I am P F C Abawimideh, Sergeant Goldman," said the soldier. "However, I have no objection to you calling me Sam."

"Okay, Sammie, baby," said Goldman.

Sam frowned.

Goldman smiled. "Again, Private, welcome to the Third Brigade of the Second Infantry Division."

The NCO looked at the vehicle and commenced reciting a memorized spiel.

"This is my M One One Three Three Stryker M E V which stands for Medical Evacuation Vehicle. It is an eight-wheeled, four-plus-four-wheel-drive armored vehicle made by General Dynamics. It is named for two American servicemen who received the Medal of Honor: P F C Stuart S. Stryker died in World War Two and Specialist Fourth Class Robert F. Stryker died in the Vietnam War.

"If you did not know, you should note, Private Sammie, that both of those men received the M O H posthumously. And even though I volunteered to spend a second year in this garden spot, that is something I do not, repeat, I do not want to do."

The new medic nodded but did not speak. Abawimideh had decided the NCO had a spiel to deliver, would not be deterred, and that interrupting it would only lengthen it.

"The Stryker vehicle is manufactured in several variants, but all have common engines, transmissions, wheels, tires, differentials, and transfer cases. We are fortunate in that both the M One One Three Zero Command Vehicle and our M E V have air conditioning units mounted on the back. Our M E V also has a higher-capacity generator.

"Our Stryker is powered by a turbocharged Caterpillar C Seven engine which is the same diesel engine used in our medium-lift trucks. The engine and transmission can be removed and reinstalled in approximately two hours.

"Pneumatic or hydraulic systems drive all the vehicle's mechanical features.

"Our Stryker's hull is constructed from high-hardness steel and bolt-on ceramic armor which protects the occupants, that's you and me and Tuck, from fourteen point five millimeter armor-piercing ammunition and fragments from one hundred and fifty-two millimeter artillery rounds.

"Our Stryker has an automatic fire-extinguishing system with sensors in the engine and troop compartments that activate one or more halon fire bottles. These bottles may also be activated by the driver, that's me, Private. Also, I can activate a C B R N Warfare system, that's chemical, biological, radiological and nuclear, which makes the crew compartment airtight and positively pressurized.

"My M E V is the primary ambulance for the Stryker Brigade Combat Team. It carries a crew of a driver and

two trauma-trained medical corpsmen. In case you
haven't figured it out yet, I'm the driver.

"My Stryker can carry four patients on standard
NATO litters or six ambulatory patients. It incorporates
automatic litter lifting devices which lift the patient to the
upper positions and locks the litter in place.

"All you have to do when the time comes, Private
Sammie, is get the patient on his litter to the back of the
vehicle, load the litter onto a tray, and push it in. The vehicle
will slide the tray over and then raise it to upper locked
position."

Sergeant Goldman looked at PFC Abawimideh. "Any
questions, Private?"

"No, Sergeant Goldman. The cadre introduced me and
several other new medics to the Stryker M E V at Fort Lewis.
Not only did we hear everything you just said all at once and
again in bits and pieces, after demonstrations we practiced
loading litters into both the right and left side trays."

"Out-fucking-standing," said Goldman. "There will
still be a fucking quiz come promotion time. A fucking
word to the fucking wise, and all that shit."

Abawimideh had questions about their patrol duties
and wondered if the nationality of a patient would affect
the destination hospital. But the young soldier wisely said,
"Thank you for the refresher, Sergeant Goldman. You
were very thorough."

A third soldier approached the pair. As with Goldman
and Abawimideh, he wore full battle gear.

"Mornin,' all," said Specialist Fourth Class Tucker
Montieth.

"It's about fucking time you got here, Tuck," said
Goldman. "This is our fresh from Forts Sam Houston and
Meriwether Lewis new trauma medic, Private Sammie
Alphabet."

Montieth looked at Sam's name tag and decided not
to correct Sergeant Goldman.

"Sam will do, Tuck," said Sam.

"Mornin,' Sam."

"Good morning, Tuck," said Sam.

"Get aboard, soldiers," said Goldman. "I've got to see if this motherfucker will start, and, if it fucking does, we'll get the fucking A C going and join the fucking parade."

Tuck and Sam climbed aboard the Stryker while Goldman got behind the wheel.

12

Millicent Goldman said Joshua, in his emails, rarely mentioned much more than the weather, what movies he had seen, what books he had read, and the need to hoard toilet paper. Often he wrote tersely: "Mom. I'm fine. Later, Joshua."

Millicent said she sent monthly 'care' packages which always included four rolls of toilet paper and a carefully packed box of homemade oatmeal raisin cookies. She said Joshua always sent a 'thank you' email which reported the number of surviving cookies. Millicent's prideful descriptions forced me to conclude she judged her packages on how many cookies reached Joshua unbroken.

When I asked, she described Joshua's three-day visit following completion of his first tour of duty in Iraq. He described his Fort Lewis, Washington, duty station and his plan to immediately return for a second tour in Iraq because "that's where the action is and where rank is made."

Millicent smiled again when she described the three days Joshua spent in her home about eighteen months before his death.

Joshua had knocked on her door one afternoon dressed in his Class A uniform and carrying his duffel bag. During the next three days he borrowed her car to shop for civilian clothes and a used Honda for himself. He told her he had completed his Army duty and had enrolled in college in Sacramento.

The fourth morning after he arrived, he bid his mother good-bye, kissed her cheek, and headed north in his Honda. He resumed his weekly email communications and reported on his apartment, his classes, and a part time job he secured at a new Best Buy store on the north side of Sacramento. Millicent described Joshua's messages as terse and said he never mentioned friends either male or female. She also said he told her he would not be able to visit her for Hanukkah because of his commitment to work the busy holiday season at Best Buy.

Millicent described taking an Amtrak train to Sacramento in late November. She took a motel room, and advised Joshua by email she would be celebrating the Festival of Lights in her room. She stayed twelve days in all, and Joshua visited her for a few minutes every afternoon.

Joshua took Millicent to his apartment one time during her trip. She said she had pestered him to see it, and she found he resided in a tiny, furnished studio apartment about three miles from the university campus.

December 10 was the last day she saw Joshua alive.

When I asked, Millicent said she did not know why Joshua decided to attend school in Sacramento.

I asked how she learned of Joshua's death.

Millicent said Detective Smith told her the police found her name and home information on a card Joshua had in his wallet.

"I took the Amtrak north," she said. "I prefer not to fly, and I did not arrive until the second morning after Joshua's death. I called Detective Smith from the Sacramento station and asked him the procedure for collecting Joshua's body. He directed me to the county morgue and said he would meet me there.

"I took a taxi to the facility. After I identified Joshua and learned what I would have to do to get his body shipped home for burial next to his father, Detective Smith gave me a box containing the clothing Joshua wore the evening he was killed. I looked in a large envelope that was inside the box and saw the items I assumed Joshua had in his pockets that evening.

"Detective Smith asked me where I was staying in case he had more questions for me. I told him I intended to go to Joshua's apartment and stay there while I packed his things and shipped them to my home.

"Detective Smith asked me if I had a key to the apartment," said Millicent. "I told him I did not, but I reached into the envelope and pulled a key ring from it.

"Detective Smith asked if he could give me a ride to the apartment and look it over. I agreed, and he drove us there in his police car."

"I was surprised to find Joshua's apartment dustless and spotless. Detective Smith and I discovered Joshua's sheets were clean and had not been slept in and his bathroom towels appeared to be unused and recently laundered.

"Detective Smith did not find that unusual as I did. When I told him Joshua had not been a particularly neat and tidy boy, the detective told me the Army forced him to be much cleaner, neater, and tidier than he had been before he served.

"When the detective found a Honda key on Joshua's dresser, we went to his designated carport and found his car there. It, too, was clean and appeared to have been recently vacuumed.

"Detective Smith suggested Joshua may have washed his clothes, his car, and cleaned his apartment during the hours before he went to that bar."

I nodded my agreement. Though I don't believe in coincidence, I saw nothing unusual about finding the clean car and apartment.

"When we found Joshua's car in its space, I asked Detective Smith if he knew how Joshua had traveled to the bar, or, if he took his car, who brought it back to his apartment. He said he did not know the answer to either question and suggested Joshua could have taken the light rail which ran near his apartment if he knew he would be drinking."

"That's planning ahead," I said.

"Detective Smith asked me if Joshua had a house cleaning service. I told him I did not know.

"Then Detective Smith asked if Joshua had ever mentioned any girlfriends to me.

"I told him no. Since Joshua had left home for the Army, he had discussed very little with me."

I nodded and sipped tea.

"I went with Detective Smith to the apartment rental office, and I listened while he asked a manager several questions.

"On the way back to Joshua's apartment, Detective Smith told me about the girl in the bar who went to Joshua as he lay dying."

Millicent paused and blinked several times. "Detective Smith said she kissed Joshua then left before the police arrived."

Millicent met my eyes. "I had to tell Detective Smith I knew nothing of the girl and no girl had contacted me."

"I'm sorry to make you recall bad memories, Mrs. Goldman," I said.

She shook her head slightly. "Before Detective Smith left, I asked where I might purchase some banker's boxes. He directed me to an Office Max. I drove Joshua's Honda there and bought boxes and tape.

"As I packed Joshua's things later that day and the next," added Millicent, "I wondered why Joshua had not told me he had a girlfriend. I considered searching out the nearest synagogue and having a chat with the rabbi. For a few moments I thought it possible Joshua might have been dating a nice Jewish girl."

Millicent interrupted herself and gave me a small smile. "I decided that would have been a waste of my time and the rabbi's time, too."

I nodded.

"I take it no young woman ever asked you about Joshua's funeral or asked for a keepsake."

"No, that did not happen, Mister Ballantine," said Millicent. "I prayed some stranger, a young woman, a college friend, an Army buddy, who had known my son well would contact me and tell me about him. It never happened."

"How long did you stay in Joshua's apartment?"

"Two additional days. After the shippers left with Joshua's property, I took his apartment key to the landlord. Then I drove Joshua's Honda here and found a buyer for it at temple."

I finished my tea while we talked a few more minutes, and then I excused myself. I felt sorry Millicent had lost her son in a bar fight, and I wondered how she might have compared that loss to his getting killed during a battle in Mosul.

I beat the thickest commuter traffic out of the heat and smog of the Los Angeles basin that Wednesday afternoon and, after climbing the Cajon Pass, entered the heat and blowing tumbleweeds of the Mojave Desert. As steady as a double axle fifth-wheel trailer is, I felt the occasional gust try to push it and my attached Jimmy into the adjoining lane as I traveled between Victorville and a chili cheeseburger which I enjoyed at the Original Tommy's near the Lenwood offramp.

As soon as I left Millicent Goldman's house, reached the freeway and a right lane cruising speed, I telephoned Harker Smith's Sacramento number. He surprised me by answering his phone.

After exchanging greetings, I asked, "I think you told me you considered the possibility one of Goldman's Army buddies is killing off the Sigma Pis?"

"Yes, I did," said Harker. "Once upon a time I did three years active Army duty my own self, and I still keep in touch with a couple of the guys I met while in uniform. But when Goldman's mother told me he never mentioned any buddies to her, I moved on.

"Why do you ask?"

"I just spent an hour or so chatting with Millicent Goldman at her home in Glendale, and she described Joshua's Army assignments," I said. "She mentioned buying and sending him a laptop computer to get him to communicate with her by email. She said he didn't write often or much, but the idea he had an Army buddy who might avenge his death entered my mind."

"It's a possibility, Dan," said Harker. "I supposed I could try to get a copy of his Army record, but, unless the Army has changed its ways, those records don't show immediate companions. I might get the names of his commanding officers through his active duty time, though, and see if I can contact them."

"Would a commanding officer know a lower ranked man in his unit?"

"Depends on the man and the officer," said Harker. "I got to know my C O when I got an Article Fifteen, that's non-judicial punishment, for gambling."

"Really?"

"A sad, sad tale, Dan," said Harker. "A guy with a double digit I Q re-enlisted and insisted on putting his re-up bonus money at risk by sitting in on our regular Friday night poker game. He snitched us off after he lost three hundred dollars. He claimed we cheated him, but we didn't unless you consider it cheating to let a stupid man with four or five beers in him lose money."

"I don't," I said.

"Four of us got Article Fifteens, a form of non-judicial punishment, which meant a loss of a week's pay and extra duty in the mess hall each night during that penalty week. With all four of us helping the regular K P crew, it never took us more than an hour each evening."

"Sad for you *and* him," I said.

"We were more careful who we let sit in our poker games after that."

"Understandable," I said, "I got nothing significant talking with Curtis Hendricks' sister, friends, or boss or from Joshua Goldman's mother, either. I'm on my way to Las Vegas to have a chat with Truman Breckinridge."

"Keep me posted, Dan," said Harker. "I appreciate your efforts, and I'll start the process to get Goldman's Army file."

"Thanks, Harker," I said. "Talk to you again soon."

The Spring Mountains west by northwest of Las Vegas contain several public campgrounds, but I knew RVers and campers seeking cooler temperatures would fill them even on a Wednesday night during the summer months. So before I left Original Tommy's, I opened my RV resort book and, on my third phone call, made a reservation for an RV space with water and electricity a few blocks east of The Strip. Because I did not know how long I would need to contact and meet with Truman Breckinridge, I paid in advance for two nights.

13

The killer had seen the Breckinridge garage door open and Truman Breckinridge's wife and children climb into a Lexus sedan. The killer concluded Truman remained home alone and decided to wait ten minutes then knock on his door and shoot him in the eye.

Six minutes later a year old GMC heavy duty pickup truck with a Nevada front plate stopped and parked in front of the Breckinridge home. The front windows each lowered two inches then a tall, lean man with light brown hair emerged from the pickup. He wore blue jeans, a long-sleeved denim shirt, and hiking boots. He turned and said something to a dog sitting in the front passenger seat.

He's got to be hot in those clothes, thought the killer.

The visitor closed the driver's door then stood next to it while holding something small and black in his right hand. He glanced down at the device then at the driver's window. After a second the visitor stepped away from the truck and walked up the Breckinridge concrete drive toward the front door.

He must not trust his remote to lock the doors. He's got to watch them work.

The man pushed the door bell then reached into his front shirt pocket and removed a business card.

Not a worker.

The killer could see the sign on the door of Breckinridge's Ford SuperDuty truck parked in front of his three-car garage: BRECKINRIDGE XERISCAPE.

Maybe the tall man guy supplies Breckinridge with rocks or plants.

The door opened, and Truman Breckinridge took the tall man's card and read it. He stood in the doorway, and the two men exchanged unheard words.

The tall man turned, started to walk away, and then stopped near his GMC pickup. More unheard words were exchanged, and then the tall man got his dog and he and the dog followed Breckinridge into his house.

It's too damn hot to sit and watch when Breckinridge has a visitor who will be there who knows how long. I'm going back to my air conditioned motel room and have a cold beer.

The killer drove a darkened minivan away from the neighborhood.

The killer had watched the large, ranch-style home the previous evening, but both Truman and his family remained inside until midnight.

The next day the killer shadowed Truman as he spent his day supervising three crews of landscapers. Except for one brief stop at a nursery where he collected several boxes of five-gallon juniper plants and a noon time drive through a fast food restaurant, he drove from home to work site and work site to work site then back home.

14

"Mister Ballantine?" asked Breckinridge after he opened his door.

"Yes," I said as I handed him an attorney card. "Mister Breckinridge?"

Breckinridge took the card but defiantly stood his ground. "You convinced me on the phone you needed to talk to me face to face, Mister Ballantine, but I don't know you." He glanced at the card, looked up at me, and added, "And I *know* I don't have any need or desire to talk to an attorney."

"Dad was right," I said. "He said light travels faster than sound which is why some people appear bright until you hear them speak."

Breckinridge frowned and said, "I'll give you thirty seconds to convince me talking with you is more important than spending time with my family."

He stood with his left hand on his door knob and his right hand on the jamb as if blocking my entry. His deeply tanned face, hands, arms, and his legs from the knees to the tops of his ankles told me he wore boots with his tee shirts and shorts while he worked in the sun. His creamy white feet and toes almost glowed above his flip-flops. I guessed he stood five foot ten and weighed about two hundred pounds.

I had stopped by his home during the cooler morning hours. His wife, Faith, told me he was working and gave me one of his cards.

When Breckinridge answered my call, he asked me to wait a moment while he got out of the sun on a shaded porch. Maybe that did not rise to what desert people would consider rude, but I felt inviting a man to one's home then not permitting him to enter and complaining about an intrusion would disappoint Miss Manners.

It annoyed me, yet I knew Kyra Simmons expected me to do the right thing. Before I left Sacramento for Huntington Beach, I had decided she would want me to advise her brother's former fraternity colleagues of his and Tyler's murders.

But my inability to suffer jerks overcame my desire to please Kyra.

"Nevermind, Mister Breckinridge," I said. I turned and stepped off his porch.

"What's so damn important you have to tell me to my face, Mister Ballantine?"

I stopped on his walk and turned to face him. "Not a thing. I'm leaving. I will not apologize for taking thirty seconds of your valuable evening, but I suggest you make sure your life insurance is up to date."

"What's that supposed to mean?"

I turned and stepped toward my Jimmy.

"Wait!" he called.

I heard him flip-flop off his porch.

I kept walking.

"OKAY!" he called to my back. "PLEASE STOP!"

I stopped near Jimmy's front bumper, and I rudely kept my back to him.

"I had a long day in the hot sun," said Breckinridge. "I'm sorry for being short with you. I'll trade you a cold beer for two sentences of explanation of that life insurance remark."

I looked at Penny sitting in Jimmy's passenger seat looking at me. "Bottle or can?"

"I only drink beer from glass," he said.

"Domestic or import?" I asked.

"Coors."

I turned and faced him. "In addition to your beer, I get to bring my dog out of the heat and into your home. Okay?"

"Will you keep him on a leash?" asked Breckinridge. "I don't want him running around inside cocking his leg on my furniture."

"He's a she named Penny," I said, "and I will keep her leashed."

"Okay."

"Then I accept your apology. I will get Penny, and you may take me to your beer."

I collected Penny from Jimmy's cab and followed Breckinridge into his house. When we were out of the Las Vegas heat, he closed the door behind us and pointed at an expensive leather arm chair.

"Please have a seat, Mister Ballantine," he called as he moved toward an opening to a hall. He stepped around a two-foot square column into a huge kitchen. A wide bar with four chrome and leather stools separated the two rooms.

I remained standing and held Penny's leash short enough she could not sit. "I forgot to ask whether your beer is Coors or Coors Light."

"I don't drink diet beer," he said.

"Good answer." I stepped to and sat in a brown leather armchair facing the kitchen. I told Penny to sit near my feet and watched Breckinridge pull two brown bottles from a huge, two-door refrigerator.

He turned to face us, placed them on the bar, found an opener, and lifted off the caps. Then he stepped back around the column and approached me with a bottle extended.

I took the bottle and long pull from it.

Breckinridge did the same and sat in a matching chair on the opposite side of a low oak table from mine.

I met his eyes. "I made a promise to help a friend, and, instead of driving north from Southern California to the Oregon coast, I took the time and spent the money to come here to tell you I think somebody wants to put a twenty-two bullet in your skull."

"What?"

"Here's your second sentence, Mister Breckinridge: Somebody murdered Jeff Sanford, Tyler Thompson, and Curt Hendricks, and I think he also plans to murder you and Michael Thomas and William King."

Breckinridge's jaw relaxed half an inch and his mouth opened slightly. "Curt's been murdered, too?"

I nodded affirmatively and drank beer.

"Will you please tell me more, Mister Ballantine?"

His voice contained a sincere plea.

"Our deal was one beer for two sentences."

Breckinridge frowned. "Some guy named Mario Martinelli told my wife, Faith, that he's the current Sigma Pi secretary. He said he'd given my home address to you. He said you wanted to talk to me about Jeff's and Tyler's murders."

"I didn't know about Curt."

"Now you do," I said. "When I finish this beer, I'll get on the road to Oregon. I want to talk to Mike Thomas as soon as possible. Face to face."

"I apologize again for being rude, Mister Ballantine," said Breckinridge. "And I have more beer."

I scratched behind Penny's right ear as I looked around the room. The furnishings reflected the high end of the price scale, and I decided Breckinridge must be doing well with his xeriscape business. I had read articles describing the scarcity of water in Las Vegas. A grass lawn had become a luxury in gated communities where the great unwashed could not gather evidence of wasted water. Middle class homeowners were tearing out their lawns and letting the desert be the desert again.

Breckinridge made an attempt at civil conversation. "I drink Coors because it's non-union beer."

"You don't like unions?" I asked.

"In my opinion, they've outlived their usefulness, and, during these tough economic times, they've lost most of their power. A guy who needs a job real bad doesn't demand union representation.

"I was a business major at Sacramento State," added Breckinridge. "I decided when I started Breckinridge Xericape, I would not deal with unions. I insist my workers show solid proof they are U S citizens, and I pay them a good wage to work in the hot sun. However, if I hear a man use the word 'union' in any context, I fire him. I have a long waiting list of guys wanting to work for me."

I understood how an employer might think that way. "I'm a sole practitioner," I said. "When I need office help, I call for a temp."

Breckinridge did not need to know I had not yet needed help in my portable office.

"You know, now that I think about it, some detective called here about a month ago. Sacramento police. I called him back the next day and answered a few questions about Jeff and Tyler and the bar fight."

I nodded and drank Coors.

"How did Curt die?" asked Breckinridge.

I decided my host might possess information I could use whether he knew it or not, and I gave him more than our two-sentence barter should have allowed. "The same as Jeff and Tyler. Somebody put a twenty-two bullet through his right eye. It bounced around inside his skull until it tore enough of his brain to destroy something necessary to life."

Breckinridge stared at me a moment then asked, "Why are you involved?"

"Jeff Sanford's parents are unhappy with the Sacramento Police Department's inability to find their son's murderer. I know a couple of cops, and I agreed to look into the matter for them. After a chat with the investigating homicide detective in charge of Jeff's case, I was about ready to present Mister and Mrs. Sanford with a cold, hard fact of life: Their son's murderer will most likely get away with it.

"Then Tyler Thompson's father, a Sacramento police officer, found his son dead with a twenty-two bullet that passed through his right eye and into his brain. The same M O as in Jeff's case. The cops went above and beyond to find Thompson's killer for one of their own. However, after many, many hours of cop time, Tyler's case has also gone cold.

"When my detective friend called me to report Curt's murder, I drove down to Huntington Beach to learn what I could and, while in Southern California, have a chat with Joshua Goldman's mother."

"That's the guy Jeff killed in that bar fight?"

I nodded. "You were there when Jeff hit Joshua with his pool cue, right?"

"I was, but I didn't actually see it. I was duking it out with some asshole Laker fan at the time."

I sipped beer and said, "I would like to hear your version of the events at the Overtime that evening."

"Jeff and Tyler stopped in our lounge area at the frat house where several of us were waiting for the Kings' game to start. Tyler announced they were going to the Overtime to celebrate Jeff's twenty-first birthday by shooting pool, drinking beer, and watching the game on a big screen. He asked if anybody wanted to join them and said he'd buy the first round.

"Several of us looked at each other and said, 'Sure.' I offered to drive, and we said we'd be right behind them.

"Which four of us did," said Breckinridge. "We drank beer while we took turns shooting pool and watching the Lakers beat the Kings.

"Pretty soon other guys were putting money on the pool table to challenge our Sigma Pi players. I don't think any of them knew each other, but they were all Lakers' fans.

"The more we all drank, the louder we all got as we cheered our favorite team.

"At some point in time during the third quarter of the game," said Breckinridge, "Goldman, we didn't know his name then, started ragging on Jeff for cheering the loser Kings. We all heard Goldman call Jeff a fag, and we all watched Jeff pop Goldman in the mouth.

"When I saw Tyler punch the guy standing next to him, I turned and put one in the gut of the closest Laker fan."

Breckinridge stopped and drank from his bottle. He smiled and continued, "That was a mistake because the guy was bigger and probably soberer than me. I was trying to float like a butterfly, sting like a bee and, more important, duck my guy's fists when Jeff whacked Goldman with his stick."

Breckinridge tilted his bottle up and down again. "When I looked over and saw Goldman on the floor, my guy got in a punch that moved my nose an eighth of an inch right of where it had been earlier in the evening. It knocked me on my ass, and I sat on the floor thinking about the great pain in my face and wiping blood off my upper lip.

"The guy that knocked me down stood over me ordering me to 'get the fuck up and fight,'" added Breckinridge. When we all heard a siren approaching the bar, he said, 'Fuck you, asshole!' and took off."

I drank beer and listened.

"I got up and stepped to the bar to get some napkins to hold against my nose. I stood there with the other Sigmas until the cops separated us to question us."

"The newspaper reports said there were several young women cheering both the pool players and the tall, sweaty millionaires running around the television basketball court," I said. "Did you know any of those girls?"

"No," said Breckinridge. "I think a couple of the Sigmas had called their girlfriends to meet us at the bar, but nobody made introductions. That may be because they trickled in after the drinking and the basketball game started. Some of the Laker guys may have been there with girls, but I'm not sure."

"Which of the Sigmas called girlfriends?"

"I'm not sure about that, either. Tyler was a local boy and had a steady girl I may have seen once or twice before. Curt was all the time hitting on anything with tits. I saw Jeff talking to a girl when he wasn't shooting pool, but, as I recall, she was sitting with the girl Curt was hitting on. I didn't know either of them."

"What about the girl who ran to Goldman while he was on the floor?" I asked. "Had you noticed her?"

Breckinridge drank beer and looked at a duck painting on the wall behind my head. Then his eyes met mine. "Oh, yes. I had. She was a hottie. I first noticed her when we entered the Overtime.

"You know how you look around and check out the possible action when you walk into a bar?"

I nodded that I did, but I did not explain that, while I notice the women, the ex-cop in me looks for males who might be less than complete gentlemen.

"Right. She was a fox. Short, dark hair. Really cute face with a great smile. Of course, she was smiling at Goldman at the time.

"Her bare arms were tanned and muscular. Her blouse was cut low on the sides and in front, and I noticed she wasn't wearing a bra on a nice, firm rack."

He grinned at me. "Maybe a tad small, but nice and firm. Know what I mean?"

"Sounds like you really gave her the once over."

Breckinridge drank more beer. "Probably about two seconds longer than I should have. As I recall, Goldman, I didn't know his name then, caught me. Rather than give me the stink eye, though, he flashed a smile that seemed to say, 'Eat your heart out, asshole.'

"I immediately realized she wasn't available and let my eyes move to another table where two other chickies sat drinking and talking. I watched Curt Hendricks move on them while I waited for my beer."

"Did the fox smiling at Goldman notice you?"

"No way." Breckinridge finished his beer, pushed himself to his feet, and headed for his kitchen. When there he looked over the bar at me and said, "She was focused on Goldman. Her smile at him was asking, 'When can we get out of here and bump uglies?'

"I don't think she saw another male in the place. Know what I mean?"

"Right," I said.

Breckinridge asked, "Ready for another?"

"No, thanks," I said.

He opened his refrigerator, fetched another non-union, glass bottled Coors, turned, and opened it. He looked at me over the bar and added, "She touched him like a lover would. A hand on his arm. Her fingers to his neck. You know?"

I nodded. "But she took off when everybody else did, right?"

"She went to Goldman and got down on the floor next to him first," said Breckinridge. "That's when we all saw what a great ass she had."

Breckinridge started on the new beer as he walked around the column and back to his chair. "I think he told her to leave."

"Why do you think that?"

"Well, I was sitting on the floor holding my nose, and I could see their lips moving. They said something to each other. I don't know what exactly, but something. And 'Get out of here, Babe.' fits.

"At that point in time I don't think anybody had it in his or her mind that Goldman would die. He'd just been wonked, you know? Knocked on his ass. He was bleeding from a cut on his head, but it was just a bar fight he had chosen to start then quit."

"Start?" I asked. "How so? I understand Jeff Sanford threw the first punch."

"Tyler and I heard Goldman call Jeff a fag and Jeff's mother a whore," said Breckinridge. "Those are fighting words to me. What about you?"

"They taught us the old 'Stick and stones …' adage in law school," I said. "Words can never be satisfactory provocation for a battery."

"Ha!" said Breckinridge. "In the *real* world of young male college students, words can start a fight. And here in the *real* west, as compared to a liberal California big city, a jury would agree."

I nodded. "That's possible."

"Jeff's use of his stick on Goldman had slowed the nearby fist fights," said Breckinridge, "but nobody had pulled knives or guns. My nose and the cut on Goldman's head were the worst wounds in the place."

15

Breckinridge looked at me and tilted his Coors bottle toward his ceiling.

"But it was serious enough most everybody took off at the first sound the cops were coming, right?" I asked.

"That's true, but that's just human nature to stay out of legal trouble," said Breckinridge. "The Sigmas stood together when everybody ran because we were fraternity brothers and had taken a pledge.

"Jeff knew he was in trouble," added Breckinridge. "While we stood there waiting for the cops, he gave his B M W key to Tyler and asked him to drive his car back to the frat house."

I nodded. "So this foxy chick you'd noticed with Goldman went to him after Jeff Sanford knocked him down with his pool cue?"

"Right," said Breckinridge. "She got her face close to his, and I saw his lips move. Then her lips moved a little, she kissed him, got up, and boogied. I figured he'd told her he'd meet her later."

Breckinridge sipped beer and added, "He didn't do that, though. While the cops questioned us somebody said he'd died in the ambulance.

"The cops got real serious after that."

"So you were in the fraternity house when Tyler invited you to the Overtime to celebrate Sanford's birthday. Did you reside there?"

"Yes," said Breckinridge. "All the guys who went to the Overtime that night did. Like I said, we were waiting for the Kings' game to start. We rode to the Overtime in two cars. Tyler rode with Jeff in his B M W roadster, and the rest of us piled into my parents' old Camry they'd given me when they bought a new one."

"Had you seen Joshua Goldman before the night of the fighting? Maybe on campus or at the Overtime some other time?"

"No. I read in the newspaper later Goldman was a Sac State student, but I couldn't remember seeing him or his girlfriend on campus. I'm pretty sure I would have remembered her if I had seen her before."

"Did you notice Goldman talking with anybody other than the girl before the fight started?"

"No. Just the girl."

"Was Jeff Sanford tight with any particular Sigma?"

"He and Tyler pal'd around together a lot. I don't know if they knew each other before joining Sigma Pi, but I saw them together a lot in the house. Like, you know, when we ate or had a party."

"Did the D A charge you with anything?"

"No, and only Jeff got arrested at the Overtime. The cops talked to the rest of us then let us go. I took the guys who had been in my Camry, and Tyler drove Jeff's car back to the frat house.

"Back at the house somebody called a former Sigma who had gone to McGeorge and become a criminal defense lawyer. He came to see us the next evening and talked with us for an hour or so. He said Jeff would probably do some prison time for killing Goldman, but he doubted the D A would charge the rest of us with anything serious. He said we might be charged with disturbing the peace or fighting in public, but he thought that would be more to scare us into cooperating than anything else."

"Did he say what he meant by cooperating?"

Breckinridge drank beer and nodded. "He predicted the D A might need a witness or two to testify against Jeff. I remember we all looked around at each other, and then Tyler asked if we could take the Fifth.

"I saw guys nodding at each other, and somebody else said we wouldn't turn on a brother.

"The attorney smiled at us and said we might change our minds if we got charged with something and the D A promised to drop the charges in exchange for our testimony.

"And," added Breckinridge, "that's exactly what happened even though we vowed, that night, to take the Fifth if subpoenaed to testify."

"According to the newspaper, Thompson testified at Sanford's preliminary hearing," I said.

"The bartender told the cops he saw Tyler punch a guy." Breckinridge drank more beer. "I guess he didn't see me punch my guy because the D A charged Tyler but not me."

"Lucky you," I said. "I take it there were no cameras in that part of the bar."

"Guess not," said Breckinridge. "Anyway, before he left that night, that lawyer told us, if we were questioned again, to say somebody hit us first and to stick to that story like stink on shit. He assured us the D A wouldn't bother with mutual combat cases.

"He also said if we did get charged with something, to plead not guilty and insist on a separate jury trial from all the other defendants. He said if we all did that, the D A would back off because of the cost."

I smiled and drank beer. "I'm sure he told you to call him if you were charged."

Breckinridge nodded. "Oh, yes. You bet he did. He gave each of us his business card, too. After he left one of the guys said the lawyer looked like he hoped that would happen." My host lifted his bottle again.

I asked, "So Tyler was the only Sigma Pi to testify at Jeff's preliminary hearing?"

"Yes, but we all got subpoenaed to be there, and we all expected to testify. We all promised each other we wouldn't rat on each other, too.

"The deputy D A whose name was on our subpoenas called the house and talked to each of us. We all later assured each other we had told him we would take the Fifth Amendment when we got on the witness stand.

"We all went to court together in my car and sat together in a back row, too," added Breckinridge. "Then the judge entered and called the case.

"After both attorneys told the judge they were ready, the deputy D A called a doctor to testify. As he walked to the witness stand, Jeff's attorney made a motion for the other witnesses to wait outside the court room.

"The judge granted that motion, and we went to the hallway and waited. After the doctor came out, a bailiff came out behind him and called the name of the E M T who treated Goldman on the way to the hospital.

"When he finished and left, the bailiff called the bartender. A guy named Colfax.

"He was in there about forty minutes," said Breckinridge. "Then he came out with the bailiff who then called Tyler's name.

"Tyler went in, and we continued to wait. We knew at that point in time the D A had charged Tyler with assault and battery. We also knew Tyler's dad was a cop, but Tyler had not hired his own attorney.

"We assumed Tyler would take the Fifth and come back out in a few minutes, but half an hour passed before he did.

"Tyler sat with us, but he didn't tell us he had testified against Jeff pursuant to a deal he had made with the D A before the hearing.

"I remember we were getting pissed because we assumed we'd be told to come back after lunch. But about ten minutes later the bailiff came out again and told us the case had resolved and we could all leave.

"We found out later Jeff's attorney cut a deal that sent him to Folsom prison for nine years."

"He was a good inmate and got out in a bit over five," I said. "Were there any hard feelings among the frat brothers after everything was said and done?"

"Like what?"

"Maybe somebody thought Jeff shouldn't have let Goldman get to him. Or maybe somebody thought Tyler should not have testified. Or somebody drank too much or argued with the Laker fans too much or punched somebody too fast."

"Not much," said Breckinridge. "I know I thought Jeff screwed up and had to pay for it. I heard a couple of guys say Tyler broke his promise not to testify, but, personally, I had no problem with him taking deal the D A offered."

Breckinridge took a drink from his bottle then added, "I knew I would have done the same thing to keep my record clean. And, with Tyler's dad being a cop, I suspected he was under a lot of pressure to keep his record clean, too.

"We all went back to our studies and stayed pretty quiet for awhile. I think some of us didn't drink quite so much beer or party so hearty for a month or two. I know I didn't. We all stopped going to the Overtime, too.

"Some of us talked about visiting Jeff in Folsom, but I never did. Tyler went out there a few times, but I don't recall anybody else saying he had."

"So much for brotherhood," I said.

"Yeah, right," said Breckinridge with a small smile.

I finished my beer and set my bottle on the table between us.

"So you and the Sacto cops think somebody is killing all the Sigmas who were at the Overtime that night?"

I nodded. "At least the Sigmas identified in the police report. Three down and three to go."

Breckinridge frowned.

"Detective Smith thinks the killer should have killed the Sigmas before Jeff Sanford got out of Folsom," I said. "That would have made for a fear factor that would have ruined his freedom."

"So you think I should be dead already?"

I smiled at his discomfort and thought, *Rudeness makes for bad karma.*

"That's logical from a revenge point of view," I said. "The only reason I can come up with for the killer waiting until Sanford's release is that he wanted to kill Sanford first. It's possible Sanford's release from Folsom triggered the killing spree, but only the killer knows for sure."

"What should I do?"

"I normally bill for my advice, Mister Breckinridge, but here's a freebie for you: Duck if you see a stranger pulling a gun."

I smiled, but he didn't. Some people don't see humor in common sense.

"I talk to strangers every day," said Breckinridge. "I buy rocks and sand and plants and drip systems, and I make written estimates on all the jobs I do. Sometimes I have to go back to a house a second time and prepare a plot plan for some homeowner's association."

I nodded.

"And lots of people carry concealed weapons in Vegas," added Breckinridge. "You know concealed carry permits are easy to get in Nevada."

I got to my feet.

Penny stood and looked up at me.

"I think that's one reason people are nicer to each other here," I said. "Nevadans have to assume everybody is packing heat. It's like Dodge City all over the state."

Breckinridge stood quickly. "Do you think the cops will catch the killer anytime soon?"

I led Penny toward the door, and, with one had on the knob, turned to look at him. "No, Mister Breckinridge, I don't think so. In my experience it is almost impossible to identify a stranger who comes to town, kills a man he doesn't know, and then leaves before the body is discovered.

"And, if that stranger is a pro somebody hired, he will be even harder to identify and catch."

Breckinridge frowned again. "Do you think I should hire a bodyguard?"

"A trained man would be another set of eyes to watch for pistol pullers," I said. "Thanks for the beer."

He nodded.

I opened the door, led Penny outside into the warm night, and closed the door behind us.

16

After making my appointment to visit Breckinridge and before driving to his home, I took a nap in my trailer. The first owner, a rich guy who used it for one family vacation then paid for indoor storage, equipped it with two air conditioners. In my previous trailer, I found I could not sleep with the unit running, but in my 'new' one I can nap on my bed over the hitch with the rearmost unit operating on low.

So, even though I had paid for a second night at the RV resort, I decided to get out of Vegas in the relative coolness of late evening.

Penny sniffed and peed while I hitched my trailer and disconnected my land lines. After checking out of the resort and topping my diesel tank at a nearby station, we left town northbound on US Highway 95.

I like the Nevada desert. I like the open spaces, the small towns one might pass through, the thousands of night stars, the sweet smell of sage, and the fact the government owns most of the state and I can park my rig almost anywhere I want. But I'm not fond of the day time desert heat in September, and I yearned to dip a four-pound monofilament line in a cool Sierra Nevada Mountains lake.

Jimmy has leather seats. In my former truck I put Penny's pillow on the floor in front of the passenger bucket. But I mellowed during the first half of my thirties, and I bought a fitted, washable cover for Jimmy's front passenger seat. Penny sits up beside me, and I let her make nose smears on the passenger door glass.

I decided she'd let me do the same if she had a truck.

She settled into a hairy, curled lump on the seat after we left the lights of Las Vegas. Before we reached the speed trap that is Indian Springs, I called Kyra on my 'new' hands-free phone.

"It's your favorite private eye, I hope, calling," I said when I heard a 'hello.' "How are you this evening?"

I heard, "I'm fine, Dan," through my speakers, "and you *are* my favorite private eye. Why do you sound like you're in a cave?"

"I'm using my hands-free phone in Jimmy's cab," I said. "Can you hear me okay?"

"Yes. Where are you?"

"I just left Las Vegas after talking with one of Jeff's former Sigma Pi brothers. Truman Breckinridge has a xeriscape business converting desert that had been turned into lawns back into desert."

"To cut water usage," said Kyra.

"Right. I'm actually on my way to Lincoln City, Oregon, to talk to Mike Thomas, then on to Tacoma to talk with Bill King.

"I usually try to call you for a date earlier in the week, but I plan to be in Reno by Sunday afternoon. Could I take you to dinner that evening? I could bring you up to date on your brother's case."

"Will you come by at the usual time?"

"If that works for you."

"It does."

"Great. See you Sunday evening."

"Good night, Dan."

I called my favorite west Reno RV resort and made a reservation for Sunday night.

If you ever find yourself near Goldfield, Nevada, and are in the mood for a free hot spring soak, you should drive north on US 95 about four miles from town and look for a sign that reads: Alkali/Silver Peak.

Turn west onto the paved but rough road and drive seven miles to a power station on the left. Just past that structure you will see trees and an abandoned swimming pool which was part of a hot springs resort a hundred years ago. Park anywhere on the flat between the two structures.

On foot you can follow the channel of water on the west side of the parking area about fifty feet up the hill. You will find a pair of brick-lined soaking tubs large enough for four or five people. Though the elevation is five thousand feet, mineral water leaves a flow pipe at about a hundred and fifteen degrees and runs into the tubs such that the water in the upper tub is hotter than the lower tub.

Penny and I reached the area about two a.m. Saturday morning. I saw a pickup with a dark camper mounted on the back and a pop-up tent trailer opened with a light on inside.

I loosed Penny into the seventy-five degree breeze and, in my trailer, pulled on a swim suit and a pair of old sneakers. I poured four fingers of Maker's Mark over ice cubes, grabbed a towel and my revolver, and walked to the cooler of the two tubs. When I found both tubs empty, I removed my suit and eased myself into the hot water.

I soaked and sipped with a wonderful view of the open desert, the star-filled sky, and the peaks on the eastern side of the Sierra Nevada Mountains.

Forty minutes later Penny had completed her explore, and I had finished my drink. I toweled off, pulled on my trunks, and led her to my trailer where we both slept soundly until eight o'clock.

I let Penny explore as I hurried through my morning routine. Then I called her in to eat some of Paul Newman's Own canned dog food while I slapped together a ham and cheese sandwich because I was not in the mood to heat a frying pan.

I ate the sandwich and drank a bottle of non-sweetened tea as I drove slowly back to Highway 95. I could have taken a dirt road short cut leading northeast from the hot spring, but I traded a gallon of diesel fuel for what I knew would be a rough ride.

At Tonopah I topped my diesel tank then headed west when US Highway 6 branched off Highway 95. Eighty miles later, at Benton, I turned west again on California State Route 120, a short cut to US Highway 395. When I reached it I turned north. After a dozen miles I slowed for Lee Vining, and, a quarter mile south of town, I turned west on 120 again as it aims at Yosemite National Park. Almost immediately I turned left into the Whoa Nellie Deli parking area for a beer and a barbecue chicken sandwich built with slices of mango.

Back on 395 I crawled through Lee Vining, along the west side of Mono Lake, then up to eight thousand plus feet at Conway Summit. There I turned left and drove the six miles to Trumbull Lake where I found a spot in the public campground.

Penny and I enjoyed three fresh trout for our dinner—one rainbow and two browns.

17—Mosul, Iraq, June 24, 2004

Sergeant Joshua Goldman raced his Stryker through the busy streets toward Avicina, the local name for Mosul General Hospital. On the NATO stretchers in the rear compartment, Specialist Tucker and PFC Abawimideh treated four car bomb victims.

All three soldiers had developed immunity to the cries of pain and screamed words they did not understand.

The medics established tourniquets to control serious bleeding, started IVs, and bandaged the most serious wounds. When the Stryker reached the hospital, they helped unload their short-term patients onto hospital Gurneys.

Goldman soon had them back on the street heading toward more victims.

A coordinated series of car bombs near police stations killed sixty-two people, many of them policemen, and injured several hundred that day. Goldman and his crew transported two dozen wounded adults and three children to Mosul area hospitals.

That evening, after cleaning and parking their Stryker, the trio shared beers in the safety of the on-base enlisted men's club.

"You guys went through a lot of fucking blood and guts today," said Sergeant Goldman. "I don't know how you fucking do it."

"We were helping people, Sergeant," said Sam.

"It's what Uncle Sam pays us to do," said Tuck. "What I don't understand is why these fuckers want to blow each other up."

"They fucking hate each other," said Goldman. "Before oil got discovered in this part of the world, they were riding around the fucking desert on fucking camels throwing spears at each other and chopping off each other's heads."

"He's right," said Sam. "They were separated into tribes back then, and each city, as it developed and grew, was controlled by a dominant tribe. They may be a bit more civilized now, but the Sunnis still hate the Kurds and vice versa."

"The private means *really, really* hate," added Goldman. "They still want to cut each other's fucking heads off with a dull fucking machete."

"I guess it's like the Bloods and the Crips back in The World," said Tuck. "Those guys are bred to hate each other, too."

"Were you a Blood or a Crip?" asked Goldman.

"Neither you honky Jew," said Tuck, "And e-fucking-nough of the stereotyping shit already. My daddy didn't leave my mama and my sisters and me. He worked hard to keep our family safe, and he neither bought nor let me wear red or blue fucking tee shirts."

"Well, fuck me all to hell, Tuck," said Goldman. "Get that fucking chip off your shoulder."

The three soldiers fell silent a few moments.

"We Americans caused part of the problem here in Mosul," said Sam. "The C I A got here first and allied itself with the Kurds. When the One-Oh-One Airborne came to town last year, General Patraeus made a civil peace agreement with the local Sunni tribes."

"I'm thinking twenty something thousand U S soldiers coming to town also pissed off the fucking Kurds because we stopped them looting the fucking place," said Goldman.

"Well," said Sam, "when Saddam's Fifth Army Corps abandoned the city two days after Baghdad fell, Kurdish fighters took control. This lowly P F C does not know why the all-knowing General gave Mosul to the Sunnis, but it's excuse enough for the Kurds to sneak back in now and then and blow up some Sunni cops like they did today."

Tuck drank beer then said, "Okay. The Sunnis and the Kurds fucking hate each other, but even though we seem to be siding with the Sunnis, I still don't think they like us very much."

Sam drank beer. "We represent a Christian country, and they aren't Christians. We've invaded their country and imposed our power on them. They don't like our religion, and they resent the fact our Christian military has the power to come in and take over."

Goldman said, "Don't forget we also helped kill Saddam's fucking sons, Uday and Qusay, here last July. I guess we'd be pissed if the fucking camel jockeys invaded the U S of A and killed Jenna and Barbara."

"Who the fuck are Jenna and Barbara?" asked Tuck.

"The fucking President's twin daughters, you moron," said Goldman with a smile. "I did a trio with them. They liked to do stuff that would make their daddy very un-fucking-happy."

"Sure you did," said Tuck. "Just like I cloned myself and the real me is sitting back home sipping Jack Daniel's and watching the Dodgers beat the fucking Giants on a sixty-inch big screen television in an air conditioned sports bar."

Sam smiled. "Don't forget we got a little pissed off when the ragheads killed three thousand of our people on nine eleven."

"That's right," said Goldman. "Pissed enough to invade their country and kill a shit pot full of them that had never heard of fucking Bin Laden much less worked for the son of a bitch."

"Fuck the ragheads anyway," said Tuck as he raised his can to his mouth.

The soldiers, having exhausted that topic to their satisfaction, fell silent. After a few minutes they opened around round of beers.

Goldman broke the silence. He pointed at Sam's name tag and said, "I like you, Private Alphabet, and you do good work, but what kind of name is that?"

"I like you, too, Sergeant Goldman, but that doesn't mean I'm willing to share a long, hot shower with you," said Sam with a smile.

"I won't ask if you won't tell," said Goldman as he brought his can to his mouth.

"To answer your question," said Sam, "My Syrian grandparents on my father's side immigrated to the U S at the end of World War Deuce. My parents and my brother and I were all born in Detroit."

"And turned that city into a fucking shit hole," said Tuck.

"I suppose you think Los Angeles is Shangri-fucking-la," said Sam.

"Torrance is close to the ocean," said Tuck.

"Detroit sits on the shores of Lake St. Clair and is close to Lake Erie," said Sam. "No salt in those waters. Unlike the Pacific Ocean near Torrance, we can drink the water in our lakes."

Goldman looked at Sam. "Yeah. Sure you fucking can. I'll bet nobody fucking drinks those waters without some serious purifi-fucking-cation first."

Sam smiled, nodded, drank beer, and said, "You got me, Sergeant. We don't even eat the fish anymore.

"But what about you, Sergeant? Aren't Joshua and Goldman Jewish names?"

"Damn straight and if you go back far enough you'll find that my ancestors cut your ancestors' guts out and used 'em for fucking guitar strings."

"Too bad they didn't have Stratocasters to put them on," said Tuck. "Jew music sucks."

"Fuck you and hip hop, too," said Goldman.

"Maybe you two assholes should wear signs that tell the local fucking camel jockeys you ain't real, pure, Honest-to-God Christians," added Tuck. "That way their snipers will aim at me first."

"All they fucking see is the fucking uniform, shit for brains," said Goldman. "Especially through a fucking rifle scope."

Sam drank beer then smiled at Goldman. "I still like you, Sergeant Goldman, even if you want to turn my guts into guitar strings."

"I'm a sergeant, Private Alphabet," said Goldman, "and I have ordered you to like me."

18

Early Saturday morning I caught five more trout, and Penny and I ate two of them with scrambled eggs for our breakfast. The other three went into my freezer.

We were back on US Highway 395 by noon and reached my favorite west side Reno RV resort five hours later. After leveling my trailer and attaching my land lines, I took a telephone call from Harker Smith.

"Not that I have any doubt," said Harker, "the Orange County lab has declared the probability the bullet taken from Curtis Hendricks' skull was fired from the same weapon that put bullets into Jeff Sanford's and Tyler Thompson's skulls is ninety plus percent."

"Won't they go any higher?" I asked. "The Nevada C S I guys are always a hundred percent sure."

Harker laughed. "This is the real world, Dan, not television.

"All three bullets got deformed bouncing off skull bone," added Harker. "The twenty-twos were soft lead and had few barrel markings left on them when they finally stopped moving. The lab people won't go beyond ninety percent."

"And won't testify to more, either," I said.

"Not likely."

"I talked with Truman Breckinridge in Las Vegas Friday evening," I said. "He believes it's okay to be rude to attorneys. My parting words, 'make sure your life insurance is paid up,' got his attention and aroused his curiosity. He even got friendly enough to invite me into his home and give me a cold Coors."

"Sounds like you scared him."

"He said he didn't know Curt Hendricks had been murdered. When I said, 'three down and three to go,' he asked me if he should hire a bodyguard."

"I'll bet he did," said Harker.

"I said another pair of eyes watching for strangers pulling pistols couldn't hurt," I said, "but I don't know if he will."

"Assuming the shooter stalks Breckinridge after killing Hendricks because he's geographically closest to Huntington Beach," said Harker, "spotting a bodyguard may force the killer to move on to another target and come back to Breckinridge later. Only presidents and rock stars can afford to pay bodyguards forever."

"I'm having dinner with my lady friend this evening to bring her up to date then I'll head for Lincoln City. I hope to warn Michael Thomas if he doesn't already have a small piece of lead in his head when I get there. Then I'll visit William King in Tacoma."

"I'm impressed with your thoroughness, Dan," said Harker. "I hope your Reno lady friend demonstrates *her* appreciation in an acceptable manner."

"Me, too," I said. "I'll keep you posted." I paused and added, "About my investigation."

"Thanks, Dan," said Harker, "and I'll call you if anything new turns up."

Over ravioli and a smooth Merlot Kyra thanked me for my efforts, and, after I told her my plans, extracted my assurance I took no time from other cases I could be working and had no risk of being killed my-own-self.

I had nothing pending. And everybody out in public runs some risk of being killed every day, most likely by a drunk driver, so I remained silent on that topic. I added I felt an obligation to advise Thomas and King of the murders of their former Sigma Pi brothers, but I did not mention I looked forward to the cooler temperatures on the Oregon coast and the predictable dampness of Tacoma.

And Kyra *did* express her appreciation later that evening.

19

Late Monday afternoon following Dan Ballantine's visit, Truman Breckinridge parked his truck on the street outside a quiet single family residence in a middle class Las Vegas neighborhood. He lifted his metal clipboard containing blank estimate forms from the area between the passenger seat and the center console and pushed his door open.

The hundred and five degree blast of dry desert heat made him hurry from his cool cab to the shaded front door. He rang the bell and hoped his customer would hurry to let him in.

Breckinridge noticed the FOR SALE sign embedded in the front lawn by a local realtor, but it did not bother him. He often xeriscaped yards to help sell houses and also xeriscaped yards for new buyers seeking to avoid usurious water rates.

While he looked around, Breckinridge decided the intense heat kept the neighbors indoors during the hottest part of the day. Nobody mowed lawns, painted fences, or tended flowers, and no children rode bicycles or batted a ball in the street.

Too damn hot to be outside doing anything, he thought. *And that includes making xeriscape estimates. I should have insisted on an earlier appointment time.*

Breckinridge noticed the existing lawn had not been getting enough water which would make it easier to remove and replace.

The killer opened the door with a naked hand and faced Breckinridge. "Mister Breckinridge?"

"That's me," said Truman.

"Ike Breckinridge?"

"No," said Truman. "Ike's my younger brother. I'm Truman. We also have a sister named Jackie. She's glad Kennedy beat Nixon."

"Interesting," said the killer. "Please come in." The killer stepped back and held the door open.

"Thank you."

Breckinridge stepped into the home and noticed an absence of furniture and pictures. White walls and beige carpet led all the way to a glass sliding door covered by an off-white curtain. Matching curtains covered the only other window and blocked a view of the next house.

Breckinridge also noticed he could not hear an air conditioner operating, felt no breeze, and the temperature inside felt close to that outside.

The killer closed the door behind Breckinridge. "My Significant Other and I are in escrow to buy this place," said the killer. "We need an estimate to take out the lawns and replace them with rocks and desert plants. The seller has agreed to pay for half the work."

Breckinridge relaxed. "I'm happy to give you an estimate." He pulled a pen from his shirt pocket and added, "And now's the time to do the lawn so you can avoid killer water bills after you move in."

"That's what we've been told. How long will it take to get the new landscaping?"

"I've got jobs lined up for about six days," said Breckinridge as he lifted his clipboard to waist level and poised his pen above it.

He did not see a small, shiny pistol move from behind the killer's back until the hand holding it was between them. Then his eyes focused on the weapon as it moved up and pointed at his right eye.

Breckinridge stared at the muzzle as his clipboard moved upward to block the bullet.

The soft *thut* was the last thing Breckinridge heard.

The killer listened to the clatter of the clipboard striking the tiled entryway while watching Breckinridge collapse. Then the killer pulled on a pair of thin leather gloves and removed the estimate form and half a dozen blanks behind it from the clipboard, folded them, and stuck them in a hip pocket.

From the other hip pocket, the killer pulled a foot-long section of pool cue. After turning Breckinridge's body onto its back, the killer jammed the stick into the corpse's right eye and leaned on it.

The killer pushed a hand into the body's right front jeans pocket and pulled it out holding Breckinridge's ring of keys. Then the killer stepped over the corpse and locked the front door from the inside.

The killer wiped the inside door knob with a gloved hand and left the house through a sliding glass patio door, stepped to Breckinridge's truck, and drove it from the neighborhood.

20

I left my east side bedroom window blinds open so the sun would awaken me Sunday morning. My drive to Lincoln City, Oregon, would take two days and make me traverse two mountain ranges: the Oregon coast range and either the Sierra Nevadas or the Cascades. I sliced a banana into a bowl of granola cereal, started my computer, and found Google Maps on the World Wide Web.

Did you know that 'google' is actually the common name for a number with a million zeros? If so, tell me how the Romans represented zero.

I like trivia. Did you know Trivia was a deity in Roman mythology? She was the goddess of sorcery and witchcraft who haunted crossroads and graveyards at night. Only dogs could see her and bark her approach.

I examined the different routes between Reno and the Oregon coast.

The shortest route, 544 miles, headed north from Reno along the east side of the mountains and cut through the Cascades at Willamette Pass just above Odell Lake. Google Maps put Odell at 350 miles away; a good day's drive pulling a trailer.

And, with a bit of luck, Penny and I could have fresh trout for supper.

Another route would take me past Burney Falls and Mt. Shasta to Interstate 5 and up through the Willamette

Valley to Eugene where I could cut west through the gentle coastal mountains. I could boondock in the Siskiyou Mountains between Yreka and Medford.

Or I could enter the Sierras west of Susanville, drive through California's Central Valley, and poke into the coast range west of Redding. I would hit the Pacific Ocean at Arcata and travel along the water for 330 miles to Lincoln City.

I thought about the weather. Other than while in the mountains, I would have uncomfortable heat outside Jimmy's cab on the east side of the mountains and in the Central California and Willamette Valleys.

Then my stomach reminded me how much time had passed since I had enjoyed fresh crab, shrimp cocktails, and clam chowder. I prefer trout fresh from a mountain lake or river, but I like fresh cod and salmon, too.

And the sooner I got to the ocean, the sooner I would enjoy cool breezes.

I finished my breakfast, hurried through my undocking routine, checked out, and drove the few blocks to Interstate 80. I headed east about ten miles, past the 80/395 junction, to the Rock Boulevard exit and left the freeway. A block north I filled my fuel tank with what I had learned was the least expensive diesel in the Reno/Sparks area.

The guy inside the store who gave me my change weighed at least three hundred pounds. I considered telling him competitive eating is not really a sport even though they televise those eating contests. I assume they do that because some viewers find watching people play poker too exciting.

I returned to I-80, drove west to the junction, then headed north on US Highway 395 toward Stead Airport, home of the annual air races where an old, bold pilot killed himself and nearly a dozen spectators who had paid to watch him fly an old, bold plane.

Nearly two hours later I rolled through Susanville, California, and, a few miles west of that town, I turned westerly on State Route 36.

I could have turned northwesterly on State Route 44 for the shortest route to Redding, my next stop, but that highway winds through Lassen Volcanic National Park. Highway 36 saved me the crawly, inattentive drivers one usually finds in national parks and the twenty dollar entrance fee.

Two and a half hours on State Route 36 took me through the Sierra Nevada Mountains to the north end of California's Central Valley. When I hit Interstate 5 I turned north and drove thirty straight and almost flat miles to Redding in half an hour.

When I spent a few days the previous Christmas holiday with my father, Lansing Ballantine, at his home in Davis, California, I described to him the majesty of the new Mike O'Callaghan-Pat Tillman Memorial Bridge, also known as the Hoover Dam Bypass Bridge, over which I had recently traveled.

Lansing suggested I stop and walk out on the Sundial Bridge over the Sacramento River the next time I passed through Redding.

So I left Interstate 5 at State Route 44 and headed west a few miles to the Sundial Bridge Drive exit. I parked in the large lot at the edge of the Turtle Bay Exploration Park, hooked Penny to a leash, and traded my cool cab for Redding's afternoon heat.

I read an informational sign declaring the cable-supported walking bridge avoided sinking pylons into the riverbed which would have, according to the writer, annoyed the nearby salmon-spawning habitat.

Tell me, Miss Salmon, are you annoyed when you are swimming upstream and come to a bridge column?

I certainly am! My ovaries are bursting with eggs, and I'm dying, literally dying, to get home and unload them. And that horny asshole that's been following me keeps sticking his nose up my wahzoo and complaining his testicles are so full of semen he's about to explode.

Then I bang my snout on some stupid concrete column those stupid humans stuck in our *river! The river my grandmother, my great-grandmother, and her great-grandmother swam before me. It's just not right, I tell you. It's just not right. Annoyed is not the word for it. 'Pissed fucking off' works much better for me.*

"I don't buy it, Penny," I said. "Fish don't have brains big enough to contain an 'annoyed' section. Even if they did, how could we tell?"

After a moment I added, "Fish probably don't curse, either."

The 217-foot tall steel pylon supporting the cables *did* look like the vertical section of a giant sundial, but it did not shade much of the bridge or me or Penny.

After twenty minutes in the hundred and two degree heat, Penny and I retreated to my rig. I stepped into my trailer, retrieved my RV resort book, then hurried to Jimmy's cab and started the engine. While we sat and let the fan blow cool air over us, I decided I would reach Lincoln City Monday evening. I called a resort near an Indian casino that advertising free wi fi, water, sewer, and electric hook ups, and a grassy dog run. The clerk said they had plenty of room and took my reservation.

The resort web page even contained a list of things one could do when one got tired of winning at the Chinook Winds Casino.

I felt confident several lucky tourists every day got so tired of winning they consulted that list for what to do next. Why else would they include such a list?

Shall we go over to the gas station and listen to the bell ring?

Shall we go sit outside the barber shop and smell the guys coming out?

Or shall we stay in this nice casino and pour our money back into these wonderful machines?

Before State Route 44 morphed into State Route 299, I suffered the heat one more time while I topped my diesel tank.

The highway started climbing before we left the commercial businesses on the west side of Redding, and, ten miles later, we drove along the north side of Whiskeytown Lake. The water looked inviting, and I could see guys in boats fishing for their dinner. But I knew the twelve hundred foot elevation would stay in the high nineties until well after dark.

The thirty miles of pavement between Whiskeytown Lake and Weaverville twisted and climbed another thousand feet into the Trinity Mountains.

I had gone online the previous evening to check for available camp sites around Trinity Lake, about sixteen miles north of Weaverville on State Route 3. As I had feared, all spaces had been reserved except for two at a private resort on the far north end of the reverse-L-shaped lake. The near three thousand feet elevation there and the opportunity to fish tempted me, but the seventy mile round trip on mountain roads would gobble too much time if I wanted to reach Lincoln City, Oregon, the next afternoon.

So I drove along State Route 299 into the Shasta-Trinity National Forest another forty miles. I found a little used paved road leading west from the main road near Burnt Ranch, and, a few miles along that road, found a dirt road leading into the trees.

Penny and boondocked in a wide spot along that road after I calculated I could make a U-turn when I wanted to leave.

Monday morning I spotted a motel with an adjoining restaurant near the junction of State Route 299 and US

Highway 101. The inn advertised free wi fi so I parked, opened my laptop, went on the World Wide Web, and Googled 'seafood breakfast in Arcata, CA.'

I hoped some nearby restaurant served lobster omelets.

Hey! Classmates.com. Will you stop with the pop-up ads, please? There's a reason I have no interest in most of the people I went to high school with twenty years ago: I didn't particularly like them then, and I haven't changed my mind. And I know what the captain of the football team is doing these days. He changes my oil and filter when I take Jimmy in for service.

Travelers must have suffered many more mediocre meals before the World Wide Web let them search for and read private party reviews. I have a tendency to trust those reviews, too, because the writers do not have to identify themselves. It's easy to write the service was crappy and the food crummy when you know you won't be back and nobody can do anything to you for being honest.

I am wary of negative criticism, but I tend to believe praise because of the effort a diner must make to find a website and put fingers to keys after a meal.

Google revealed zero cafes serving seafood for breakfast, and only one, several miles south in Eureka, which had received better than average reviews for its regular breakfasts.

I checked eateries in Crescent City, about eighty miles up the coast, and found a highly recommended café 'where the locals eat.' All but a few of the fifty-five reviewers gave the place four or five stars.

 The establishment did not post a menu online, minus a point in *my* opinion, but I had already decided I did not want to scramble my own eggs that morning.

US Highway 101 hugged the coast thirty miles then turned inland for a fifteen mile trip through Prairie Creek Redwoods State Park. Why anybody named a creek 'prairie' in that forest I do not know, but the giant red trees made for a nice change of scenery.

After another few miles along the Pacific Ocean, Penny and I entered Crescent City, found our target café, and parked. I let Penny sniff a few minutes, promised her a treat, and entered the cozy eatery.

My waitress frowned at my request for a lobster omelet, but she assured me the cook prepared a 'very good' Denver omelet.

He did, and I broke my promise to Penny by eating every bite.

The final minutes of light before sunset Monday evening found Penny and me sitting in an ocean breeze outside my trailer. I enjoyed a comfortable camp chair and had my feet up on the bench seat of the provided picnic table. Penny seemed to enjoy the close cropped grass next to my chair.

After docking, I had hiked the short distance to the casino. Inside, I walked past a deli, a busy buffet, a steak house, and, finally, a sea food restaurant which I entered. After my waiter assured me the rockfish had been caught locally within the previous twenty-four hours, I ordered it and a glass of the house white wine to follow a spinach and blue cheese salad.

I could have paid my bill in 'player points' if I had possessed any, but, since I planned to deduct the expenses on my income tax return, I used a credit card.

Back in the RV resort I opened a bottle of Two Buck Chuck, which is so good I do not know why anyone would pay more for wine, and read *The Oregonian* newspaper I had purchased in the casino.

My ringing phone surprised me. I did not recognize the calling number, but I knew the 702 area code covered Las Vegas.

"Hello," I said.

"Is this Mister Dan Ballantine?" asked a female voice I did not recognize.

"Yes."

"This is Faith Breckinridge, Mister Ballantine. We talked briefly last week, and I believe you visited my home and talked with my husband, Truman, last Friday evening."

"We did, and I did. What can I do for you?"

"Is Truman with you now?"

I detected anxiety in Faith's voice.

"I'm sitting in a camp chair in a Lincoln City, Oregon, R V resort, Mrs. Breckinridge," I said. "Truman is not with me."

"Oh. Okay, thank you. I thought perhaps he had agreed to talk with you again and forgot to tell me he was meeting you. I'm sorry to have bothered you."

"That's okay, Mrs. Breckinridge," I said. "Did Truman mention the reason for my visit?"

"He said one of his former fraternity brothers had been murdered in Sacramento, and the family had hired you because the police could not solve the case."

"That's not all of it, Mrs. Breckinridge. I don't mean to alarm you, but I suggest your next call should be to the Las Vegas Police Department."

"Why, Mister Ballantine? Truman sometimes works after normal business hours making work estimates for prospective customers."

"But he's not answering his phone, is he?"

"No," she said softly. "He's not."

"In fact, Mrs. Breckinridge, not one but three of Truman's former fraternity brothers were recently murdered in similar ways. While I had some questions for Truman, an additional reason for my visit was to warn him I believed the killer may come after him, too.

"I'm here in Lincoln City to give the same warning to Michael Thomas who was one of the other Sacramento Sigma Pi members."

After five seconds of dead air, Faith said, "Truman didn't tell me all of that. I guess I will call the police. Thank you, Mister Ballantine. Good-bye."

I closed my phone and stared at it. For a moment I remembered the time a professional assassin named Mako Fazan searched for me with homicide in mind. I later learned Fazan had been paid a million dollars by a Russian criminal I had caused to be arrested to murder me before I could testify at his trial.

He was to receive another million dollars when he could prove my death to the Russian.

I had traveled through several states before he found me and aimed a Colt Single Action Army revolver at me while I aimed my Smith & Wesson pistol at him. The difference in the weapons, single action versus double action, may have saved my life.

I opened my phone and punched Harker Smith's number. When I heard the beep I left a message: "Dan Ballantine calling. It's eight fifteen Monday evening. I just took a call from Faith Breckinridge, Truman's wife, who thought, no, hoped, her husband had failed to tell her he was meeting with me for a second conversation.

"I told her I am presently in Lincoln City, Oregon, Truman is *not* with me, and I urged her to call the Las Vegas Police Department.

"There's no need to return this call, Harker, but I would, of course, like to hear from you if Truman has lead in his head."

26

My drive Tuesday morning to the address Mario Martinelli had given me for Michael Thomas took me across the world's shortest river. The Devil's River flows westward one hundred and twenty feet from Devil's Lake to the Pacific Ocean. The local Indians named the lake from a legend which declares a giant fish, or some other type of monster water creature, would occasionally break through the lake's surface and scare everybody.

It must have been a very flat monster because the Devil's Lake is only twenty-one feet deep at its deepest point.

Still in Lincoln City, I crossed the river and soon turned east on SE Devil's Lake Road. Jimmy did not change direction, almost due east, but, within a mile of US Highway 101, the two-lane blacktop changed its name to NE Devil's Lake Road.

I wondered who decided that changing point and what prompted it.

A few blocks later the road *did* angle northeasterly, and I said, "They need to move that sign, Penny."

We passed through Devil's Lake State Park and followed the shoreline on the east side of the three-mile long lake. As the Devil's Lake is only a third of a mile wide, I could look across it in some places and see the homes on the west side.

I turned left on Sheltered Nook Road and parked in front of what I hoped was the Michael Thomas residence.

When I rang the door bell I heard a dog start barking inside the house. A big dog from the sound of the bark. The volume increased as the dog neared the door.

Soon the door opened and a young woman, bent over to hold back a now quiet German Shepherd by its collar, twisted her neck and head to look up at me. "Yes?"

I held an attorney card toward her.

She took her hand from the door handle long enough to take the card, but she put her hand back on the handle without reading it.

"I am Dan Ballantine. I would like to talk with Michael Thomas."

"He's not here."

"Does he live here?"

"Yes, but he and Kathy are on an Alaskan cruise," said the young woman. "I'm house sitting for them."

The German Shepherd must have decided I presented no threat or his curiosity about why I smelled like a dog overcame his aggression. He lowered his head, strained forward, and tried to sniff my jeans.

I looked down at the dog and said, "My dog is in my truck. Your Shepherd probably smells Penny on me. It's okay to let him get closer."

"He's not my dog," said the young woman as she bent lower and let the Shepherd get close enough to touch my knee with his nose.

"When will the Thomases return from their cruise?"

"Two weeks from last Sunday," she said without looking up at me.

"Thanks," I said. "I'll stop back by after they return."

"Okay," said the woman.

She straightened, pulled the dog back, and closed the door.

"Well, dern, Penny," I said as I slid behind Jimmy's steering wheel and started the engine.

Penny stepped on the center console and sniffed my right pants leg.

When I had made my Lincoln City RV resort reservation, I asked for two nights because I calculated Michael Thomas might not be available to talk to me until the evening hours. While I retraced my drive back into town, I decided not to ask for a refund for the second night. I wanted another fresh sea food dinner.

And I wanted to shop. Well, buy. Real men don't shop.

I had noticed earlier, when I turned from Highway 101 onto SE Devil's Lake Road, a mall of factory outlet stores on the southeast corner of that intersection. On the return trip, I pulled in, found a shaded space, and parked.

Oregon has no state sales tax, and the factory outlet stores are supposed to have discount prices, right? Well, maybe not the latter, but my underwear supply was due for replacement. I bought ten new ones at the Jockey store.

My "new" fifth-wheel travel trailer has a small clothes washer and dryer stacked one above the other. I read once that doing one's laundry in a public laundry facility costs about the same as purchasing the machines and doing it at home. The difference is the convenience factor. At home one can start a load and do something else while it washes.

I used to buy fifteen packages of underwear which required me to find a laundry business every two weeks or so. Now I can start my generator and my clothes washer and drive down the highway if I wish.

How's that for multi-tasking?

I found my size at the Levis store and bought three.

I had traveled through Pendleton, Oregon, a month earlier on my way to Joseph. I would have stopped at the *real* factory outlet store there, but I expected a guy who had faked his death for his life insurance money to reach Joseph shortly after I did. So I did not take time to stop, and I felt pleased to find and buy a colorful wool shirt/jacket at the Lincoln City Pendleton outlet store.

Some people might consider walking through the Coach, Eddie Bauer, Columbia, American Eagle Outfitters, and Rockport stores shopping, but, since real men do not shop, they would be wrong.

I did not find anything I could not live without. I gave some thought to a reasonably priced pair of hiking boots in the Bass store, but my Danner Mountain Lights had at least one more rebuild in them.

"Are you up for a hike, Penny?" I asked when I returned to my truck.

When I checked in, the RV Resort had given me a 'Things To Do In Lincoln City' brochure. Because I assumed Michael Thomas would be at work during the day and I would have some free time, I had loaded my small back pack with water, cheese, crackers, trail mix, a first aid kit, and a light poncho in case it rained. My Smith & Wesson forty-four special revolver, in case I met a small, angry momma bear that might try to keep me or Penny from getting too close to her cubs, sat holstered in my right hip pocket.

I drove south on US Highway 101 from the outlet stores to SE 48th Place where I turned east. The street soon morphed into South Schooner Creek Road. After climbing into the coast range about ten miles, I turned north onto Drift Creek Road and soon reached the Drift Creek Falls Trail parking lot which contained zero other vehicles.

The 'Things To Do' brochure declared I would need a National Forest Recreation Day Pass before I placed a single boot on an Oregon trail. I had found the U.S.

Department of Agriculture website and blown five dollars for a document I could download and print.

I wondered how many officiously observant forest rangers would be on the trail to check my pass.

I let Penny out, retrieved her collar and leash from under my seat, slipped into my backpack and Tilley hat, locked Jimmy, and set out on Trail Number 1378 which immediately descended into lush forest. The hike offered great views and the state's longest suspension bridge, two hundred and forty feet, which hovered a hundred feet above Drift Creek. From the bridge I had a view of eighty foot Drift Creek Falls.

I washed down half of my trail mix with canteen water before starting back. Penny got a few nuts but no chocolate bits.

We saw not a single forest ranger the entire hike.

My phone rang as I carried my new underwear and jeans into my trailer about four o'clock.

"Good afternoon, Detective Smith," I said. "How are you today?"

"I'm well, but Truman Breckinridge is not."

"Oh?"

"I called Las Vegas homicide first thing this morning and played your message for them. The department had done nothing with Faith Breckinridge's missing person report yet which is, I'm sure you know, S O P for the first twenty-four hours.

"Following my call they put out an A P B for Truman's truck," added Harker. "Because it has his name on the doors, they found it in a supermarket parking lot before noon. He wasn't in it, but the killer, I'm assuming it was the shooter, left Truman's keys in the ignition. We're lucky somebody didn't steal the truck and plan to burglarize his home with his house key."

"I assume L V P D found no hairs, fibers, or prints."

"You assume right. Faith found Truman's work schedule, and Las Vegas homicide started questioning his crews. One helpful foreman said Truman left his worksite about four Monday afternoon with the advisement he had to go make a landscape estimate. The good news is that Truman mentioned the street name to the foreman."

"But, I assume, not the house number."

"That's the bad news," said Harker. "For L V P D, not me. They supposedly knocked on forty doors before they found him."

"Dead and with a section of pool cue protruding from his right eye, right?"

"You private dicks are so smart," said Harker.

"A lucky guess."

"The house had a For Sale sign out front. The cops found a broken bedroom window and an unlocked sliding glass door. They think the shooter went in the first and out the second. He must have called Truman for an estimate then invited him in when he arrived. The cops found the corpse lying on the entryway just inside the front door."

"I have a recording which contains my warning to Truman that the killer might be coming his way. I assume he didn't hire a body guard."

"If he did the guy wasn't on duty yet," said Harker. "L V P D is examining Truman's cell phone records and the inside of his skull as we speak."

"According to a house sitter, Michael Thomas and his wife are on an Alaskan cruise and won't be home until a week from Sunday," I said. "I plan to drive to Tacoma tomorrow and see if I can find William King. Hopefully I can beat the killer to him.

"Say," I added quickly. "There's a thought. If the killer is flying from target to target, he'd have to check his gun with his luggage. Is it worth asking the airlines for their gun carrying records?"

"I doubt he's dumb enough to make a record of his travels, Dan," said Harker, "but I'll run your question by Lieutenant Steele."

"You're probably right," I said. "He's traveling in something inconspicuous. Perhaps I will reach Tacoma before he does."

"Let's hope King takes your warning more seriously than Breckinridge did."

"Yeah," I said. "Let's hope."

I thought about my phone conversation with Harker while I put away my new clothes.

If the killer traveled from target to target by motor vehicle, I doubted he had yet reached Lincoln City *or* Tacoma.

I opened my computer and went to Google Maps. The shortest route from Las Vegas to Lincoln City covered 995 miles and required an estimated eighteen hours. I assumed that travel time did not include toilet or food breaks, heavy traffic, or speeding arrests.

The shortest route from Las Vegas to Tacoma was over eleven hundred miles with twenty hours travel time.

"Come, Penny, come," I said.

I drove us back to Michael Thomas' house, rang the doorbell, and listened to the German Shepherd bark his way to the door.

The dog continued to bark as I rang a second, and, two minutes later, a third time.

While I stood at the door I wondered if the killer had arrived and murdered the house sitter. It *is* possible to drive a thousand miles in twenty-four hours. The Iron Butt Association certifies the Saddle Sore 1000 (1000 miles in 24 hours), the Bun Burner 1500 (1500 miles in 36 hours), and the Bun Burner GOLD (1500 miles in 24 hours) for their motorcycle riding members.

But I decided the killer had no need to drive against a clock. The house sitter probably drove into Lincoln City for a pound of hamburger or dental floss or something.

I pulled an attorney card from my pocket, reluctantly printed my cell phone number and 'Please call me ASAP' on the back, and stuck it in the door jamb.

I drove back to town and stopped at a store advertising fresh fish. The counter man told me he bought the ling cod from a fisherman just off his boat at ten o'clock that morning so I purchased a twelve ounce filet so I would have enough to give Penny a few bites.

My mutt watched closely as I grilled the ling cod over hot briquets. She got her bites while I ate mine with a serving of previously frozen peas.

Penny does not like peas, frozen or otherwise.

After cleaning my plate and utensils, I pulled my RV book and looked at resorts in the Tacoma area.

The house sitter did not call, and I did not sleep as well as I usually do that night.

Since I did not know if room existed at the end of Sheltered Nook Road to reverse direction while towing a medium-sized fifth-wheel travel trailer, I drove Jimmy solo back to the Thomas house after breakfast. As I walked to the door, I noticed my card remained where I had left it.

I pulled it, rang the bell, and listened to the barking dog.

Then the door opened, and the house sitter, bending at the waist and holding the German Shepherd by his collar, looked up at me.

I said, "I'm sorry to bother you again, Miss, but has anybody else been here asking for Mister Thomas?"

"No." She struggled to hold the hundred pound dog.

"It's okay to let the dog sniff me," I said.

She took one step forward.

"I don't mean to alarm you," I added, "but I am involved in a case in which four men have been murdered recently, two in Sacramento and one each in Huntington Beach, California, and Las Vegas. The man in Las Vegas was murdered Monday afternoon at about four o'clock.

"All four of these men were members of the Sacramento State University branch of the Sigma Pi fraternity six years ago. Mister Thomas was also a member of that fraternity at that time.

"If anybody you don't know comes here asking for him, I urge you to call me," I said as I handed her my 'aged' card. "I came back last evening and left that card in your front door jamb."

She took the card, did not read it, but said, "I had to run an errand, and I entered the house through the side door when I returned."

"Okay, but it's important you call me, Miss. Or, if you don't trust lawyers, call Detective Sergeant Harold Smith of the Sacramento Police Department."

She looked at me without expression.

"Did you hear me say somebody murdered a Las Vegas man Monday?"

"Yes."

"Well, I personally visited that man at his home last Friday evening and warned him somebody might be coming to murder him."

"You did?"

"Yes," I said. "Then I drove here to warn Mister Thomas. And I plan to leave within the hour and drive to Tacoma to warn another man who was a Sigma Pi member six years ago.

"Will you promise me you will make that call if anybody you don't personally know wants to talk to Mister Thomas?"

She nodded. "Yes, I will, but I'm not opening this door to anybody else until Mike and Kathy get home."

"That's wise," I said. "Just look through the peep hole and call me if anybody you don't know comes to the door. Or call Detective Smith. Harold Smith. Sacramento Police Department. Do you want his number?"

"I'll call you," she said. "If you don't answer, I'm sure I can get his number. You said 'Sacramento Police Department,' right?"

I nodded. "Detective Smith is in the Homicide Division."

"Got it," she said.

"Thanks, and I'm sure Mister Thomas will thank you after I talk with him which I hope to do as soon as he returns home."

"Why are you driving all over the place? Why not just call people?" she asked.

"The current Sigma Pi secretary would only give me addresses," I said. "I would have called with a warning if I had had Mister Thomas's telephone number, but I would have visited, too. I like to talk to people face to face, and I'm hoping one of the Sigma Pis will remember something that will help me identify the murderer."

"Well, I would give you Mike's number, but he doesn't have his phone with him. Kathy, his wife, she's my sister, told me she wanted a vacation far away from electronic devices. She said she would make Mike leave his laptop and smart phone home, and they are both on his desk in the den."

"Do you want Kathy's number?" she asked. "I know she took her phone because she's called me three times already and sent photos she took from the ship."

"No," I said. "That's not necessary. Mister Thomas is safe as long as he is not here. I wouldn't interrupt their vacation with this sort of information. It's not good news, and I don't want to ruin their trip. It can wait until he returns."

She nodded. "Okay, but I'll tell them about your two visits while I drive them home from the airport."

"Three visits," I said. "I plan to return to Lincoln City a week from Sunday. I will stay in the R V resort near the Indian casino. Please tell Mister Thomas I can be here ten minutes after he calls me."

"I'll do that," she said. "If I go on line, do you think I can read about those other murders?"

"Yes. They've been published in the *Sacramento Bee* and the newspapers in Huntington Beach and Las Vegas," I said. "And, in my opinion, neither you nor Mrs. Thomas have any reason to be afraid. The killer has specific targets. As far as I know, he hasn't killed anybody not on his Sigma Pi list."

22

While sitting in a darkened vehicle near the Devil's Lake at the end of Sheltered Nook Road, the killer had watched the Michael Thomas house through binoculars since first light.

Three other vehicles had left three other homes on the block, but nothing had moved at the Thomas house.

The arrival of the same Nevada-plated GMC pickup truck containing the same tall man that had visited the Truman Breckinridge home in Las Vegas surprised the killer.

What the hell? What is he *doing here? Why did he talk with Breckinridge? Why is he talking with Thomas?*

Is he a cop?

Damn!

23

Less than an hour after my morning visit to the Thomas home, I had hitched my trailer, made a second reservation and checked out, and put Lincoln City in my rearview mirrors.

US Highway 101 had angled inland at the north end of town, and, a few miles later, I turned east on Oregon State Route 18. The highway through the Siuslaw National Forest section of the coast range took an hour then the road straightened as it aimed at the Willamette Valley and Portland.

In McMinnville I rolled by a sign describing the Evergreen Aviation and Space Museum as the home of the Spruce Goose.

My father, Lansing Ballantine, is a history professor at the University of California at Davis. He is also a movie buff, and he purchased a DVD copy of *The Aviator* which he declared was a reasonable account of Howard Hughes' activities from the mid-1920s to 1947.

We watched it together at his home one evening, and when I expressed interest in Hughes, Dad loaned me a biography.

I found Howard Hughes a fascinating guy if a bit of a nut job near the end of his productive life. As an attorney I enjoyed the curious legal battle to probate his estate which was worth more than a million dollars to the lawyer assigned the task. Hughes owned real property and had a movie office in Los Angeles, he had lived atop a Las Vegas hotel which he had purchased when they asked him to leave, and his primary businesses, the Hughes Tool Company and his personal Tran World Airlines office, had been in Texas.

Most people believed he died in an airplane over Mexico so Texas, Nevada, and California fought the legal battle to handle his estate.

The Spruce Goose's frame, a nickname Hughes supposedly detested, was constructed primarily of birch.

I made a note to visit the museum on the way back to Lincoln City after I talked with William King.

I neared Interstate 5 about one o'clock, topped my diesel tank, and then aimed my rig north. I rolled through Portland and across the Columbia River. Three hours later, when I-5 hit Washington State Route 16 on the south side of Tacoma, I turned west and drove eleven miles to Gig Harbor.

Unimpressed with the small Tacoma RV parks described in my book, I had made a reservation at a well-reviewed resort in Gig Harbor.

When I checked in the clerk recommended I try The Tides Tavern or The Green Turtle for a sea food dinner. She assured me they were both excellent, but, when I asked if I would have to change clothes, she said the Tides would be happy to serve me wearing almost anything.

I followed a bowl of clam chowder 'made fresh daily' with broiled halibut and a local ale. Good stuff.

24—Mosul, Iraq, November, 2004

At the end of the first week, insurgents commenced a series of coordinated attacks and ambushes designed to take control of the city.

On the eighth day of the month, the 1st Battalion, 24th Infantry Regiment, the "Deuce Four," battled determined and coordinated insurgents around the Yarmuk traffic circle in the heart of western Mosul. Bravo Company's 2nd Platoon sustained nine casualties and had two of their four Stryker vehicles rendered useless by RPGs.

At the same time the 3rd Battalion, 21st Infantry Regiment, the "Gimlets," got hammered on the north side of the city with small arms, RPGs, and machine gun fire.

The next day an Army major and an Air Force master sergeant died as a result of an RPG and mortar attack on Forward Operating Base Courage.

On the tenth, insurgents flooded the streets and secured the initiative. By the next day they had captured one police station and destroyed two more after they distributed all the weapons, ammunition, and flak jackets they could find. The Iraqi police force scattered and deserted from the street fighting.

The Deuce Four and the Gimlets coordinated a hammer-against-anvil plan which, with the help of U.S. Air Force jets dropping JDAM bombs, regained the north side of town.

Insurgents attacked nine more police stations on November twelfth. They destroyed one and took control of the other eight. They also attacked and burned to the ground the Kurdish Democratic Party headquarters.

2000 Peshmerga fighters requested by the Iraqi Defense Ministry arrived in Mosul on the twelfth, and the U.S. Air Force began a bombing campaign on rebel positions which lasted into the next day. However, by the thirteenth the insurgents controlled two-thirds of Mosul and began to hunt down members of the Iraqi security forces. Those they found were publicly executed—often by beheading.

The Americans diverted the 1st Battalion, 5th Infantry Regiment of the 25th Infantry Division from Fallujah to help retake Mosul. An Iraqi Special Forces battalion from Baghdad was called in to assist. 300 members of the Iraqi National Guard were transported from the Syrian border.

On November fourteenth insurgents took two more police stations and burned the Ninewah Provincial Governor's house.

Over the next three days the combined anti-insurgent forces slowly regained control of the northern, eastern, and southern sections of Mosul. The insurgents managed to make a safe haven of the western part of the city from which they continued to conduct hit-and-run attacks over the following months.

Sergeant Goldman, Specialist Montieth, and PFC Abawimideh enjoyed little sleep during the battle for Mosul. They employed their Stryker vehicle every day and most nights transporting injured U.S. soldiers, Iraqi security forces, Kurdish Peshmurga fighters, and the occasional civilian to hospital facilities.

An insurgent RPG struck the right front side of a small car parked behind the team's Stryker just as Montieth and Abawimideh approached it carrying a stretcher. Tuck and Sam were both knocked off their feet, and the stretcher they carried spilled their patient, a young Peshmurga fighter.

Sergeant Goldman, standing on the left side of the Stryker, felt the blast and small pieces of metal strike his legs as he watched Tuck and Sam drop the stretcher they carried and fall to the pavement.

Goldman ran to Tuck who had been closest to the explosion and found blood flowing from several wounds in the young soldier's legs and arms. Tuck's helmet and flak jacket had protected his head and back.

"TUCK!" called Goldman.

Tuck did not respond.

"God damn it!" said Goldman. He felt for a pulse in Tuck's neck and felt a strong and steady pumping.

Goldman hurried to Sam and found similar but fewer wounds.

"SAM!" called Goldman.

PFC Abawimideh's eyes opened and slowly focused on the sergeant.

"Ow! That hurts," said Sam.

"Move your arms and legs!" said Goldman.

Sam complied with the order.

"You'll live," said Goldman. "Tuck's unconscious. Can you help me load him into the Stryker?"

"I think so," said Sam. With a grimace, the young soldier stood.

"Pull one of the stretchers!"

Sam looked down at the wounded Peshmurga fighter still on a stretcher. "We should load this guy, too."

"Fuck the raghead," said Goldman. "You and Tuck have priority."

"Okay, Joshua, but we can't leave him."

"We won't. Pull a stretcher for Tuck, damn it!"

While they moved him, Tuck opened his eyes and looked at Goldman.

"I'm hurtin,' Sarge," said Tuck. "Real bad."

"We're moving out now, Tuck," said Goldman. "Hang in there."

The NCO and Sam loaded the foreigner then Sam collapsed to the pavement unconscious.

Goldman knelt next to Sam and noticed a growing blood stain on the young soldier's inner thigh. He quickly removed Sam's combat gear and tightened a belt around the wounded soldier's upper leg. Then he lifted Sam onto the Stryker's floor and closed the rear hatch.

Goldman knew of a nearby Mosul hospital, but he drove as fast as possible to a U.S. facility. He called ahead on the radio with the advisement he was bringing two wounded American soldiers, one with a serious bleeder, for treatment.

At the hospital Goldman lifted Sam and carried the unconscious soldier toward the door.

A pair of medical corpsmen ran to the NCO with a stretcher.

"This soldier is a bleeding from a wound on the inner thigh," said Goldman.

"I see it," said a medic. "Shrapnel probably nicked an artery. We'll get on it stat."

Goldman saw Sam's eyes had opened, and he walked beside the stretcher to the building. "You're gonna make it, Sam. We're at the hospital already. They're waiting for you in there. You'll be in surgery in a few minutes."

Sam smiled. "Thanks, Sergeant. I want to see your face again when I wake up. Okay?"

"I'll be here, Sam," said Goldman. "I promise. And I'm putting you in for a medal."

"Don't do that," said Sam softly. "I'm no hero."

"I'm getting you a Purple Heart, soldier, whether you like it or not."

"Just be here when they get done with me, okay? I'll need a ride."

"You've got it, Private. You've got it."

Goldman found Tuck's eyes open as he and a third corpsman unloaded his stretcher.

"I'm fucking hurtin' all over, Sarge," said Tuck.

"You've got lots of little shrapnel wounds in your legs and arms, Tuck," said Goldman, "but it's all tiny little shit, and you're gonna be okay. We're here at the Army hospital already."

"What the fuck did you say, Sergeant?" asked Tuck. "I can see your lips moving, but I can't hear your fucking words. In fact, I can't hear shit."

Goldman looked up at the hospital medic. "Let's get him inside."

"I'm with you, Sergeant," said the medic. "And don't worry about his hearing. Most of the time the loss is temporary. He'll have his ears back before his shrapnel wounds have healed."

"I hope you're right," said Goldman. "It's way too fucking soon for him to get a ticket home."

25

I arrived at the address Martinelli had given me for William King at ten o'clock the next morning. The middle class neighborhood reflected care. Houses and fences carried fresh paint and green lawns got regular mowing. A next door neighbor trimmed a hedge between his and King's house.

When nobody answered the doorbell, the neighbor called, "They're not at home, mister. They both work during the day."

I looked his way. "Thanks. I'll leave a note."

I pulled an attorney card and jotted my cell phone number on the back. I also printed: I need to talk to you about the Sigma Pi murders.

I stuck the note in the door jamb and stepped toward the neighbor.

"Do you know if William King usually enters his house through the front door? The last note I left on another front door got ignored because the tenant entered through a side door."

"I'd stick my card in the side door here, too," said the older man. "Bill and Bella, Isabella, both work at McChord. They commute together. When they get home they park in the garage in the back and enter through the side door off the driveway."

"Thanks," I said. "I'll move my card."

"Is there some emergency?" asked the neighbor. "I can get in touch with them if necessary."

"No. No emergency," I said. After two seconds, I asked, "You haven't seen any other strangers knock on their door in the last day or two have you?"

"Nope, but I spend most of my time indoors." He smiled. "We're retired, but my wife does volunteer work at a day care center. She sometimes asks me what I did during the day. I always say, 'Nothing, but I didn't finish. I've got more to do tomorrow.'"

I smiled.

"She's been thinking about quitting, though, 'cause it's getting harder and harder for her to keep up with the little kids. And I'll tell you this, Mister, I'm not looking forward to having her around all day. I like to watch sports on television. She says she'll watch with me, but I predict she'll start complaining about five minutes later."

"Not a Seahawks fan, huh?"

"Not the Seahawks, the Mariners, the Sounders, the Thunderbirds, the Stealth, the Force, or the Huskies, either."

"I know the Huskies and the Mariners, but not the others."

"The Sounders play major league soccer, the Thunderbirds play ice hockey, the Stealth is in the National Lacrosse League, and the Force is a rugby team," he said. "We also have a Pacific Coast Soccer team, the Crossfire, the Rat City Rollergirls, roller derby, and the Grizzlies, an Australian Football League team."

"Always something on then," I said.

"Almost."

"Well," I said, "my dad says women who claim to like sports must be treated as spies until they demonstrate solid knowledge of the game and the ability to drink as much beer as the males present."

The man smiled then glanced at his watch. He looked up at me and said, "Nice jawing with you, mister, but the Mariners' game starts in a few minutes. See you later."

"Go team," I said as I turned toward Jimmy.

William King called me a few minutes after six that evening. "I found your card in my door, Mister Ballantine. What's this about Sigma Pi murders?"

"Did Mario Martinelli call you?"

"No. Who's Mario Martinelli? What's going on here? Why would an attorney want to talk to me?"

I paused a moment because I detected either anxiety or a short temper in King's voice. "Which question should I answer first?"

"What about the Sigma Pi murders?"

"Your name, Mister King, along with Jeff Sanford, Tyler Thompson, Curt Hendricks, Truman Breckinridge, and Mike Thomas, appeared in a police report and several *Sacramento Bee* newspaper articles following the death of Joshua Goldman in the Overtime sports bar about six years ago."

"Yeah, so?"

"Sanford, Thompson, Hendricks, and Breckinridge have all been murdered within the last three months," I said. "Because of the similarities in their deaths, the police believe the same man murdered all of those former Sigma Pi members.

"The Sanford family hired me to find Jeff's murderer after the police put the case on a back burner.

"Hendricks and Breckinridge have been murdered since I got involved."

"I remember all of those guys," said King, "but I haven't kept in touch with any of them. I also recall talking with a Sacramento police detective a month ago, but you still haven't told me who Mario Martinelli is."

"I prefer to have these conversations face to face, Mister King," I said. "May I return to your home or meet you in some public place?"

"I got burned by a lawyer once, Mister Ballantine, so I no longer talk to them," said King. "I'll check out what you've told me, but I can't think of any reason I need to talk to you."

"If you change your mind, I will be in town until ten o'clock tomorrow morn ... ."

I heard the connection break.

My father tells me people have not always been so rude, and he places the blame on technology.

In one of his lectures, Lansing describes a telephone party line to his students. He says that, as a boy, he would occasionally hear a faint *bing* from the sturdy, black, phone company owned machine. He confesses he would occasionally lift the receiver and listen to a neighbor's private conversation.

I was a fifteen year old high school student when Clarence Thomas suffered what Lansing called a 'grossly intrusive inspection.' This undesired scrutiny came as part of Thomas' nomination to the Supreme Court.

I recall my father telling me he was appalled that investigators subpoenaed and published Thomas' video store rental record. He said, "I suppose discovering a man rented porn movies every evening might say something negative about him in some people's minds, but I think it stinks that any person can be inspected that closely."

Lansing also found invasions of the privacies of President Bill Clinton and Monica Lewinsky which followed Paula Jones' sexual harassment suit against Clinton to be extraordinary and outrageous.

I was a college student when Clinton got impeached, and my father expected me to intelligently discuss the issues of the day with him when we got together. He also expected me to have an opinion and to voice a reasonable defense of said opinion.

I found it easier to agree with Lansing than to oppose him. However, as a law student and in the intervening years, I have watched the Supreme Court narrow the definition of impermissible searches and expand the scope of search warrants. Like my father, I doubt the founding fathers would approve the current limited state of personal privacy.

But, then, I doubt Washington, Jefferson, Adams, Paine, and Franklin would believe the existence of cyberspace and our ability to observe people and places in real time. We can see satellite views of nude beaches and study restaurant menus. On the other hand, though unseen, our electronic footprints remain forever and can be tracked by persons with authority, power, or the right equipment.

Hacking into private phone calls closed Rupert Murdock's London newspaper, but the reporters got away with listening to private conversations for a long time before they were caught.

While I think technology can solve problems, I doubt there will ever be a total and reliable safeguard of our electronic privacy. Every time somebody comes up with a solid wall, somebody else pokes a hole in it.

Lansing and I agree on one thing: Whenever one is out in public, one should assume one is being watched and recorded.

William King may have believed his refusal to talk to lawyers helped safeguard his privacy, and I, as a lawyer, could not disagree with him. I drove back to my RV resort and took Penny for a long walk around our temporary neighborhood.

William King called me a few minutes before nine o'clock that evening.

"We are willing to discuss these murders with you, Mister Ballantine," he said, "but we prefer to meet in a public place."

"Who is 'we,' Mister King?" I asked.

"My wife and I."

"Do you know The Tides Tavern in Gig Harbor?" I asked.

"Yes."

"I'm parked in a nearby R V resort, and I enjoyed a Full Scale Ale there last evening," I said. "If you and your wife would meet me there, I could enjoy another."

"We'll be there in twenty minutes."

26

The Harmon Pub & Brewery of Tacoma brews the Full Scale Ale, a Best Barrel Bitter, and a Peninsula Porter for The Tides Tavern. I usually ask a saloon server what the establishment has on draught. When I am unhappy with the choices, I order a bottle of Corona. My Tides Tavern waitress had suggested the Ale, and I agreed it tasted good.

I had a cold glass in hand when a mid-twenties couple approached my booth.

"Mister Ballantine?" asked the man.

I stood. "Yes. If you are the Kings, please join me."

"We are," said the man. "I'm Bill, and this is my wife, Isabelle." They sat and slid into a relatively light level of privacy.

I relaxed and took my seat.

Isabelle was not cute. She wore no make-up I could see. Her eyes were two millimeters too far apart, her nose was a hair too wide, her eyebrows over-plucked, and her thin lips gave her a stern demeanor.

Listen ladies, men don't care much what you do with your eyebrows. Do you have two of them? Okay. We're done. Leave them alone.

The worst thing about Isabelle, though, was half an inch of dark roots against her medium blond hair.

I do not understand why so many women think they must be blond, but, in my opinion, if one bleaches her hair she must keep it bleached down to the roots all the time. There is nothing fashionable in phony light hair with real dark roots, and it tells me the woman is lazy.

The guy who told Bill about Isabelle probably said, "She's got a great personality."

Lansing tells me popular music went into the toilet when disco appeared a few years before my birth. Until I reached my teens I listened to Golden Oldies because that's what Lansing listened to. I rebelled as a teenager, of course, and listened to Madonna, Tommy Page, Lionel Richie, Bon Jovi, and Bruce Springsteen. The Boss's *Born to Run* was the first album I purchased, and I still listen to him.

But the others have faded. I don't often listen to music while I drive, I prefer recorded books, but the original purchaser of my GMC took advantage of a special XM radio offer when he bought the truck. When his widow sold Jimmy to me, she told me it still had fifteen months of satellite radio available. I have discovered I prefer the 50s, the 60s, and Elvis to most other stations.

I think I will not pay to extend the subscription when it expires. I have enough CDs to keep me happy.

I was about twelve years old, and I remember I laughed aloud when I first heard Jimmy Soul sing *Never Make a Pretty Woman Your Wife*. Lansing had insisted I help him repaint my bedroom, and he had turned his portable radio to the oldies station.

"Listen to the lyrics, Dan," he had said. "There's wisdom there. When you start dating girls, I predict you will find, as I did, the high maintenance females are often more concerned with their appearance than their relationship with you.

"If you find yourself with a girl who constantly plays with her hair or checks her appearance in every window you pass, it's time to move on."

"Okay, Dad," I had said but I must not have had sufficient conviction in my voice.

"I'm serious, Son," added Lansing. "The true test of a woman is to take her camping. See if she'll crawl into a sleeping bag and sleep on the ground in a tent in the woods. She if she can survive away from toilets and restaurants without griping. Look for one who will pull her hair back away from her face, put on a baseball cap, brush her teeth from a cup of ice cold canteen water, and, without complaining, squat behind a bush to pee."

I had laughed.

"Believe me, Dan," said Lansing. "A woman who will camp with you is a prize."

Several years later, after splitting a bottle of wine with me, Lansing confessed I was conceived in a tent near Thousand Island Lake on the John Muir Trail.

I never took my wife, Jamie, camping. Our marriage lasted less than two years. It ended when she placed our severely autistic infant son in my arms and drove away after saying, "I can't take it anymore."

So I did not fault Bill King for marrying a plain woman, and, as we conversed, I decided Isabelle possessed intelligence, wit, and she demonstrated care and concern for her husband.

She also got points for asking me what I was drinking and ordering the same while Bill ordered diet cola. A woman who will drink a beer with you immediately looks better than one who won't.

I looked at Bill after our waitress left with our drink orders. "Did you know that when Coca Cola appeared in 1886, it was advertised as an Esteemed Brain Tonic and Intellectual Beverage?"

"No, but I feel smart for ordering one."

Bella smiled and said, "The diet version doesn't help the brain, Bill."

I smiled. "I'm sure they mentioned that in the blurb I read."

"Next time I'll order a Mai Tai," said Bill.

I frowned at him, but I did not feel it appropriate to remind Bill in front of his wife that the Man Rules permit the ordering of fruity alcoholic drinks only when: 1. One is sunning on a tropical beach, and, 2. Only when it will be delivered by a topless model, and, 3. Only when it is free of charge.

"So who is Mario Martinelli?" asked Bill.

"The current Sigma Pi secretary, Sacramento State University division," I said. "He gave me addresses but no phone numbers. He also told me he would advise each of you he had done so."

"I have not yet heard from him, but I don't think Sigma Pi has my most recent number," said Bill, "and, like many other people, we discontinued our land line several years ago."

"Have you visited other former Sigma Pi members?" asked Isabelle.

I nodded. "Kyra Simmons, a personal friend and Jeff Sanford's brother, asked me to look into Jeff's murder after the police put the file into the cold case drawer. She did not know Tyler Thompson had been a Sigma Pi member with her brother.

"I hoped the other people present at the Overtime the night of the brawl might tell me something the police missed," I added, "but before I could start contacting them, Curtis Hendricks was murdered in Huntington Beach."

Isabelle sucked a small breath and looked at Bill. "I remember Curt Hendricks well," she said. "He was an annoying flirt who always looked at my chest when he talked to me."

"I've heard the flirt accusation from other people," I said. "I drove to Huntington Beach from Sacramento to talk to the city employee who found dead Curt sitting in his truck in a beach parking lot. I also talked with his sister, a pair of his buddies, and a not-too-cooperative employer.

"Then I drove to Glendale and interviewed Joshua Goldman's mother. He's the man Jeff Sanford killed with his pool cue in the Overtime saloon."

Bill nodded. "I was served with a subpoena to testify against Jeff at a court hearing. So were those other guys. We went to the court house together as a show of unity, and we had vowed to take the Fifth Amendment when questioned.

"But it never came to that for most of us," added Bill. "We waited in a court hallway all morning while others testified. Finally Tyler Thompson got called in, and then, on the advice of his private attorney, Jeff agreed to a plea bargain which got him eleven years in Folsom Prison for voluntary manslaughter."

I nodded. "He got out early for good behavior."

"That's good," said Bill. "I always thought his sentence was too harsh."

"I was too late to talk to Hendricks," I said, "but I drove to Las Vegas and had a chat with Breckinridge. He told me about the subpoenas, your joint pledge, and the group of you Sigmas waiting in the hallway.

"Three days after I talked with Breckinridge, he was murdered in the same manner as the others. A small caliber bullet in the right eye."

Bill stared at me.

"Really?" asked Isabelle. "Did you tell him three of his fraternity brothers had been murdered like that?"

"I did," I said and shifted my gaze to her.

"Ignoring you wasn't very wise," she said.

"I've discovered it's easier to get older than it is to get wiser," I said.

Bella nodded and sipped ale.

"I stopped by Lincoln City on the way here to warn Mike Thomas, but he and his wife are vacationing in Alaska. I plan to head back south and be there when they return."

"Didn't Breck, that's what we called him back then, think you were serious with your warning he may be a target?" asked Bill.

I looked at Bill. "I thought so. Just before I left his home he asked me if he should hire a bodyguard. I agreed that was a good idea."

"We can't afford that," said Bill.

Isabelle looked at her husband. "Maybe not, but we both have several weeks of unused vacation time. Perhaps we should go see my family while the police and Mister Ballantine try to find this murderer."

Bill looked at her then at me.

"I'm Dan," I said, "and Isabelle has a good idea, Bill. If the killer can't find you, he can't kill you."

"True," said Bill. He sipped from his glass.

Isabelle smiled at me. "Please call me Bella, Dan, and I want to thank you for telling us all this."

Her lips got even thinner when she smiled, but she had great teeth, honest warmth, and suddenly her twinkling eyes weren't too far apart nor her nose too wide.

I nodded and smiled back at her then looked at Bill as he set down his glass.

"It's not a convenient time," he said.

Bella put a hand on Bill's forearm. "It would be inconvenient for me, honey, if you were murdered."

Bill looked at her but said nothing. Then he lifted his glass again and sucked down a few more gulps of dark, carbonated liquid.

Bella drank beer.

When Bill looked at me, I asked, "Where were you in the Overtime bar when the fights started?"

"Bella and I were sitting alone at a small table," said Bill. "I had called her from the frat house before we left and asked her to meet me at the Overtime. She knew some of the guys, and I doubted I'd be staying as long as they would. She had a V W, and I figured she could give me a ride back to the house."

"Bill wasn't a big drinker as a college student, Dan," said Bella.

"I couldn't afford it," said Bill. "Not in a bar, anyway. I joined Sigma Pi partly because I don't like to cook, and I could live and eat there cheaper than on my own in an apartment.

"And even today a six dollar beer in a bar like this doesn't taste nearly as good as the same beer for a dollar at home."

"I agree," I said. "I think that's why so many Corona commercials show a guy and his girl sitting on a beach staring at an empty ocean."

Bill nodded. "I remember I had put my three dollars on the table then shot a crappy game of pool when my turn came. When I finished, I sat down and suggested to Bella we leave after I finished my beer which, if I recall correctly, was my second. I could see the trouble brewing between the Sigma Pis and a bunch of guys cheering for the Lakers. Everybody was getting louder, both the Sigma Pis and the Laker fans, and the pool playing was getting too expensive."

"The cost to challenge a pool game had risen to a whopping five dollars," said Bella.

Bill looked at her. "Back then that was expensive to a poor college student."

Bella smiled at her husband then looked at me. "The Sigma Pis weren't really a bunch of saloon fighters, Dan. They drank quite a bit in the frat house, but they were actually a pretty studious group, and they collected jackets for the local poor kids at Christmas time.

"I met Bill in an Art History class, and our first date was to the Crocker Museum in downtown Sacramento." She smiled at Bill and added, "We still visit museums together."

I looked at Bella. "Did you see the young woman who went to Goldman after Sanford knocked him down?"

"No." She shook her head. "The instant the fighting started, Bill told me to leave. I remember asking him to come with me, but he said he would stay with his brothers."

Bella looked at Bill and added, "I remember admiring his loyalty at the time." She looked at me. "Of course, nobody expected Goldman to die, but I left the parking lot before the police arrived."

"And I lied to the cops," said Bill. "I told them I did not know the name of the girl I had been talking to. I didn't want to get Bella in trouble with her parents who did not approve of me."

Bella patted Bill's forearm. "They like you now, honey."

Bill looked at Bella, and they exchanged smiles. "I'm sure they'll like me more when we give them a grandchild."

"You've got that right, and we should do it," said Bella with a warm smile for her husband.

I drank some of that good beer. When they looked at me, I asked, "Can you think of anybody who showed a serious dislike of Sigma Pi when you were in it, Bill?"

Bill shook his head. "No. There was some rivalry with the other fraternities, of course, but I can't imagine anybody hating us enough to hunt us and murder us six years later."

"You might give it some more thought," I said, "because somebody is doing just that."

"We went on line and read about the recent murders of the four former Sigma Pi brothers, Dan," said Bella, "and I don't think somebody hates the fraternity members. I think the murderer is seeking revenge for Joshua Goldman's death."

"I can't disagree," I said, "but other than his mother and that girl in the Overtime saloon the night his death, I have not been able to find a single person who even knew him. The Sacramento homicide detective told me he will try to get Goldman's military records and identify his buddies, but that's a slow process.

"Before Sergeant Smith can identify men Goldman served military time with, the killer could finish murdering the Sigma Pis involved in the Overtime bar fight and disappear."

"That's sad," said Bella.

I nodded. "The next time you go on line, look up the statistics for solved murders when the murderer does not know the victim. It may be sad, but it's a fact of life most of them are successful."

27

After walking with Penny, and then building myself a chopped onion and cooked crab omelet the next morning, Thursday, I studied my maps. As I finished my coffee, I thought about what I should do with eleven days before I wanted to return to Lincoln City.

I noticed Olympic National Park on my Washington state map, and, when I did an online study, I found Lake Crescent within the Park supposedly contained Beardslee trout, a cousin to the rainbow. Ten or so miles from the lake, the Sol Duc Hot Springs listed several pools and a nearby camp ground on the Sol Duc River.

I made a reservation for that evening, undocked, checked out, and headed south toward Interstate 5.

I could have gone north from Gig Harbor, but that route would have necessitated a ferry ride near Port Gamble. I would also have missed the scenic section of US Highway 101 from Shelton to Gardiner.

Jimmy's phone rang as I drove along the west side of Dabob Bay just north of Brinnon.

"Ballantine," I said.

"This is Hailey Evanston calling, Mister Ballantine. I'm Kathy Thomas's sister."

"Hello, Miss Evanston. What can I do for you?"

"A man just came to the front door," said Hailey. "I didn't open it, but he yelled he was looking for Michael Thomas."

"Can you describe him?" I asked.

"I would say he was between twenty-five and thirty years old. He was African American. About five foot ten. I'm afraid to guess his weight, but he was not fat. He looked fit. His black hair was cut short on top and even shorter on the sides."

"How was he dressed?"

"He wore a dark blue business suit, a white shirt, and a maroon tie," said Hailey. "He looked like some sort of salesman.

"I wasn't afraid of him, Mister Ballantine, but I did not open the door."

"If you planned to kill someone, would you want him to take one look at you and be afraid?" I asked.

"Uh, no, I guess not."

"Where did he go after he left the door?"

"I watched him until he walked away, and I saw he wore shiny black dress shoes."

"Any facial hair?"

"No."

"Did you see his eyes?"

"I did," said Hailey. "I think he decided nobody was home except Rinty. Just before he walked away, he stepped close to the peep hole and tried to look through it. I didn't want him to suddenly see light instead of dark, so, when his face was about a foot away, I closed my eyes and pressed my forehead against the peep hole. That way when he looked in he couldn't see anything."

"Good thinking," I said. "Did you see anything in his hands?"

"Yes. When he walked away from the porch. He carried a thin, white bag like the kind you would get at the grocery store. It had something in it heavy enough to make it sag below his knees, but I couldn't see what."

"No bible?"

"No. I don't think he was a church guy. Those people usually leave a 'Come to Our Church' or 'Are You Going to Heaven?' brochure hanging on the door knob when they leave."

"Did he say he wanted to speak to Mister Thomas for any particular reason?" I asked.

"No," said Hailey. "In fact, he didn't really say anything. All he did was call Mike's name loudly two times about a minute apart. Then he walked away.

"Rinty was barking the entire time, and I didn't try to stop him."

"Did you see the man go to a vehicle?"

"No. He turned and walked along the road like he intended to visit the next door neighbor, but I couldn't tell if he did looking through that tiny peep hole."

"So you don't know whether he went next door or to a vehicle parked nearby."

"No," said Hailey. "Sorry. Rinty was barking, and I tried to quiet him after the guy walked away. I thought about looking through a window, but I would have had to peek through the blinds. I didn't want him to know anybody was home in case he was watching the house as he walked away."

"Thanks for calling, Miss Evanston," I said. "If it would make you feel better, call the police and report the visitor."

"That would mean I would have to tell them about you and the other murders," said Hailey.

"Probably," I said. "I have no problem with you telling them about me or giving them my card. If they call me, I will refer them to Detective Sergeant Smith in Sacramento."

"Well," said Hailey, "the guy could have been a salesman or somebody Mike knows. I think I'll wait to see if he comes back. If he does, I'll call the cops then."

"That's okay, too," I said. "Please call me again, too, if he returns."

"I will."

"Thanks again, Hailey," I said. "I appreciate your help."

I rolled a few miles and thought about Hailey's call. Then I telephoned Harker Smith and reported what she had told me. He reminded me no police agency had found any witnesses to any of the Sigma Pi murders, but said he would prepare a transcript of my call and forward it to the other cops.

Then I called and left a message on Kyra's recorder. I needlessly advised her she need not return my call, told her I was still chasing down Jeff's Sigma Pi brothers, had nothing significant to report other than Truman Breckinridge's murder which she could Google if she wanted the details, and concluded with the advisement I would not return to the Reno area for at least two weeks.

And so I spent ten days in far western Washington and the northwest corner of Oregon. Fifteen dollars got me seven consecutive days in Olympic National Park, and fourteen dollars per day got me a primitive RV space in the forest along the Sol Duc River near the hot springs.

For three days I drove to and fished Lake Crescent during the early morning hours. Back at my trailer I fixed breakfast then walked to the hot springs pools. I had my choice of ninety-nine degree mineral water in the wading pool, one hundred and four degree mineral water in the medium pool, one hundred and one degree water in the large mineral pool, and eighty degree water in the fresh water pool.

I almost expected to see an empty pool for people who did not want to soak.

One afternoon a rain storm passing through my section of Olympic National Park gave Penny and me free showers as we walked to my trailer from the medium mineral pool.

Penny and I enjoyed short hikes into the forest, and we ignored the restaurant, the café, and the gift shop.

On the fourth day I towed my trailer through light rain to Lake Crescent and fished until I had three nice trout. I cleaned them, stuck them in my reefer, and drove to US Highway 101. There are no public roads through Olympic National Park, so I looped westerly and then drove out of the storm as I turned southerly around the western border. Penny and I re-entered the Park at its southwest finger near Lake Quinault located, nicely enough, in the Quinault Rain Forest.

The lake, though in a U.S. national park, is owned by the Quinault Indian Nation. I assumed the tribe got a cut of my original fifteen dollars and the daily fees I paid to park in a lakeside camp ground. I also had to purchase a fishing permit from the tribe which would have annoyed me had I not caught plenty of trout.

Another storm rained out our second day at Lake Quinault so Penny and I enjoyed a leisurely drive on the thirty mile loop around the lake. I noticed private homes on the north side which I thought unusual for a national park.

The next day I pulled my trailer about a hundred and twenty miles down US Highway 101 to an RV resort on the Southwestern Washington coast. I paid for full hookups so I could dump my tanks.

After undocking Jimmy, I backtracked a few miles to the Willapa Wildlife Refuge which contains salt marshes, muddy tide flats, rain-drenched old growth forests, isolated sandbars, coastal dunes, and beaches. While wandering through the visitors' center, I heard an announcement that Ranger Ingram would give his morning talk in ten minutes.

Almost without exception I have found the local experts know their stuff, and they have usually delivered their nature talks enough times to make them interesting. Ranger Ingram was even better. His silver hair and friendly smile evidenced a sense of humor and years of experience and knowledge.

Ingram described the flora and fauna then focused on the amazing numbers of birds in the area as they have no place to go except over the wide Pacific Ocean if they fly farther west.

When he mentioned owls living in the Willapa forests, he said, "I'm sure you all know it's a *herd* of cattle, a *flock* of chickens, a *school* of fish, a *gaggle* of geese, and a *pride* of lions.

"Did you know it is an *exaltation* of doves?"

When he got no response, he asked, "Does anybody know the proper collective noun for a group of owls?"

Nobody did.

"It's a *parliament* of owls.

"One last group," added Ranger Ingram. "We don't have any baboons in Willapa, and that's a good thing. Baboons are the loudest, most dangerous, most obnoxious, most viciously aggressive, and least intelligent of all primates."

Ranger Ingram smiled and added, "A group of baboons is called a *congress.* I wonder where they got that one."

While in the area, I visited Cape Disappointment with its oldest functioning lighthouse on the west coast. In 1788, English Captain John Meares searched, unsuccessfully, for the Columbia River which had not yet been named. He named the jutting point for his failure. Four years later American ship Captain Robert Gray found the river and named it after his vessel.

I crossed the four mile long Astoria-Megler Bridge into Oregon in bright sun light on Saturday morning.

Thick fog would be intimidating. I drove through Astoria and found a rebuilt Fort Clatsop five miles southwest of the town.

Lewis and Clark and their men camped there, well, at the original, not the replica, during the winter of 1805-1806. They named it after a helpful local Indian tribe that, after frequent prior exchanges with European traders and explorers, found little value in the cheap trinkets offered by the American explorers.

I had difficulty imagining spending a wet, cold winter in such small quarters.

28

The killer had located a safe place to park and had watched the Michael Thomas residence through a small telescope each evening from five o'clock until the house went dark about ten thirty.

The killer noted the house sitter walked the German Shepherd on a leash from the side of the house to the open area at the edge of the Devil's Lake at nine thirty every night. She carried plastic bags with her and usually returned swinging a bag of fresh dog poop.

When Michael Thomas failed to appear by the end of the week, the killer guessed he might be on a business trip or a vacation. With that in mind, the killer commenced surveillance of the Thomas home at ten a.m. on Saturday and Sunday mornings.

Shortly after parking and erecting a telescope on a tripod in the back of a darkened minivan Sunday morning, the killer watched the house sitter back a white Ford F-150 pickup alongside the Thomas house and into the street. The killer noted the German Shepherd in the rear section of the crew cab truck.

The pickup returned six hours later, and the killer noted two additional persons in it. The house sitter sat behind the steering wheel, a second young woman sat in the front passenger seat, and Michael Thomas sat in the rear section with the dog.

29

"Mister Ballantine?"

"Yes."

"Michael Thomas calling. My sister-in-law, Hailey, tells me you want to talk with me. She said you said my life is in jeopardy."

"It is, Mister Thomas," I said.

"What makes you think so?"

"I prefer we have a face to face conversation, Mister Thomas," I said. "I'm staying in an R V resort near the Indian casino. I can be at your home in ten minutes."

"My wife and I are very tired from our flight from Fairbanks and a long drive from the Portland airport, Mister Ballantine," said Thomas. "And I have to get up and go to work in the morning. Could we have this conversation tomorrow evening?"

"We could, Mister Thomas, but please understand the police and I believe your life is in danger now. Right now. We believe the killer has somehow obtained the addresses of all the Sigma Pi members who were at the Overtime saloon the night Jeff Sanford killed Joshua Goldman.

"The killer may be watching your home as we speak."

After a moment of silence, Thomas said, "Okay, Mister Ballantine. I am adequately alarmed, but I need to take Hailey home. Could you come by around eight o'clock?"

"I'll be there, Mister Thomas," I said. "See you then."

Michael and Kathy Thomas reflected a long day of travel from Fairbanks to Seattle to Portland to Lincoln City. They had no explanation why Alaska Airlines did not fly directly from Fairbanks to Portland, and they complained about a two hour layover in the crowded SEA-TAC airport.

They listened politely while I described the murders of four young men Michael had known while attending Sacramento State University. But Michael had few questions for me, and I left with the feeling the Thomases may have been too tired for a meaningful conversation.

The Kings had suggested a vacation to hide from the killer; the Thomases wanted to sleep.

30

Half an hour after the house sitter, the dog, and the other two people arrived, the killer watched Michael Thomas, the house sitter, and the dog leave the residence in the Ford truck. Thirty minutes later Michael and the dog returned without the house sitter.

The appearance of the tall man in the GMC truck a short time later surprised the killer. When the tall man left the house fifteen minutes later, the killer lowered the telescope to the floor, moved to the front of the vehicle, started the engine, and followed the GMC at a discreet distance.

When the GMC turned into the RV resort, the killer drove to the casino and parked. Twenty minutes later the killer walked through the RV resort and noted the GMC truck with Nevada plates parked next to a fifth-wheel travel trailer.

The killer then walked to the casino, entered the minivan, and drove back to Sheltered Nook Road.

31

Ten minutes after nine o'clock that evening, Michael Thomas with his leashed German Shepherd, Rinty, beside him, walked from his home to the end of Sheltered Nook Road. He loosed Rinty to sniff and stood on the shore staring at the Devil's Lake's calm water. He pondered Dan Ballantine's warning. He hated the fact he had enjoyed a carefree cruise up the Inland Passage and a week touring Alaska only to come home to the possibility somebody wanted to kill him.

Rinty saw a fish jump for a bug which had landed on the water's surface and barked at it.

"Quiet, Rinty," said Thomas.

Rinty ran into the water until all four legs were wet then stopped. He backed from the water and ran back and forth along the narrow beach as if searching for a path to the fish.

What does one do if somebody wants one dead? thought Thomas. *Never leave his house? Go into hiding?*

I have obligations and commitments, he thought. *I can't become a hermit at home or any other place.*

Thomas turned when he heard approaching footfalls crunch the rocky part of the shore.

The killer approached Thomas in the gathering darkness.

"Nice evening," said the killer with a smile.

"Yes," said Thomas.

The killer suddenly brought a gloved hand holding a suppressed pistol into the space between them.

Thomas froze at the sight of the shiny weapon.

The killer aimed at Thomas' right eye and pulled the trigger.

Thomas collapsed to the shore.

As the killer rolled Thomas' cooling corpse onto its back, Rinty came close and sniffed at his master. He then looked at the killer, bared his teeth, and growled.

The killer shot the dog in the head then forced a ten-inch section of pool cue into Thomas' right eye socket.

The killer stood erect, looked around, and then turned and walked along Sheltered Nook Road toward NE Devil's Lake Road.

32

A few minutes before ten o'clock Sunday night, someone knocked on my trailer door.

Penny barked, and I traded my Kindle reader for the Smith & Wesson revolver sitting on a small table next to my recliner. While most people would step to their door and put an eye to the peeping lens, I knew the door would not stop a bullet. I stepped to a window and moved the blind a quarter of an inch away from the glass.

At the sight of a uniformed police officer, an experienced man with sergeant's stripes on his sleeve, standing near my trailer with his right hand on his holstered pistol, I stepped to my phone, opened it, and dialed 9-1-1.

"This is the emergency operator," said a female. "What is your emergency?"

"This is Dan Ballantine calling. I am in a travel trailer in an R V resort near the Chinook Winds Casino. A man in a police uniform just knocked on my door, and I am wondering if he is real."

"Just one moment, please," said the female.

I moved back to my window and watched the officer step to my door, knock with his left hand, and call, "Are you there, Mister Ballantine?"

I looked toward my door in a feeble attempt to throw my voice. "I am here. I have just called emergency to see if you are really a police officer."

"I am Sergeant Sutter, Mister Ballantine," said the man in the uniform. "Chief Boone wants to talk with you in his office."

Just then a male voice came from my telephone. "This is Lincoln City Police Chief Andrew Boone, Mister Ballantine," said the voice. "Kathy Thomas found her husband and her dog dead at the end of her street a short time ago, and I would like to discuss the matter with you. Would you accompany Sergeant Sutter to my office, please? You are not under arrest."

"Certainly, Chief Boone," I said.

I put my revolver in a drawer, told Penny to stay, stepped from my trailer, and locked the door behind me.

"May I pat you for weapons, Mister Ballantine?" asked Sergeant Sutter.

"I don't think that's necessary, Sergeant Sutter," I said. "I'm reaching into my pocket for my Swiss Army knife, and I assure you that's the only item that could possibly be called a weapon on my person."

Sutter placed his right hand on his holstered semi-automatic pistol. "Please hand the knife to me."

He took it in his left hand and placed it in his left front pocket without looking at it.

"Chief Boone expects me to pat down all strangers, Mister Ballantine," said Sutter.

I decided not to go to war over the issue. I spread my legs and extended my arms from my sides.

Sutter's pat was light but thorough.

"This way, Mister Ballantine," he said then waved his left hand toward the resort office.

I didn't like Sutter. As I stepped as directed, I said, "Those stripes must be new."

Sutter said nothing.

I spotted a black and white patrol sedan parked near the RV resort office and stepped to the front passenger door.

Sutter stepped around me and opened the right rear door. "Please sit in here, Mister Ballantine."

"No, thanks, Sergeant Sutter," I said. "I wore the uniform and patrolled on the graveyard shift for the L A P D a few years back. I know how nasty back seats in patrol units can be even if they look clean.

"Chief Boone has invited me to his office as his guest. He specifically told me I am not under arrest. If I cannot ride up front with you, then I will call him and ask him to visit me here. Not only will I not pat him for weapons, I'll offer him a beer."

Sutter's face muscles tightened, and he gave me his hard stare.

"Don't think about it too long, Sergeant," I said, "and there's no need to get jawed up with me. I'm one of the good guys, and, as such, I refuse to sit in the back where you put the pissers and pukers you hauled to your jail before you made sergeant."

Sutter closed the back door and opened the front passenger door.

"Thank you, Sergeant," I said. I climbed into the seat and fastened the belt.

We did not engage in pleasant banter as we traveled the short distance to the police station. Inside Sergeant Sutter directed me with another wave of his left arm through a solid door toward the office area in back.

The four offices were separated by glass walls and were empty except for the farthest. I saw a man in civilian clothes get to his feet.

"In here, Mister Ballantine," he called. He added, "Thank you for coming," as I led the sergeant toward him.

I could read the backwards *Chief Andrew Boone* painted on the glass top half of the open door. I entered, stepped to a nice oak desk, and extended my hand. "Dan Ballantine," I said.

Chief Boone, in his mid-thirties, shook my hand while Sergeant Sutter stepped around me and placed my pocket knife on the Chief's desk closer to the officer than to me.

"Nice to meet you, sir," said Boone. "It's just a formality, but may I see some identification."

I slowly pulled my wallet, removed my Nevada driver's license and my Nevada and California bar cards and handed them to him. While I did so, Sergeant Sutter stepped back around me and stood in the open door. When I glanced at him, I noticed he rested his right hand on his gun butt.

I smiled at him.

When I looked back at Boone, I saw him frown at my bar cards. That usually happens when a cop discovers I am an attorney.

Boone handed me my cards. "Let's sit, Mister Ballantine."

We did. He pulled my pocket knife closer to him and examined it.

"Is this a clock?" he asked.

"Yes," I said. "With an alarm and a stop watch."

"Amazing," he said. "How often do you have to replace the battery?"

"I don't know. I've had it one year, and it's still running," I said. "I rarely use the alarm, though."

He looked up at me and handed me the knife. "Please tell me what you and Michael Thomas talked about when you visited him earlier this evening."

The chief interrupted my narrative at one point and telephoned the Sacramento Police Department. He identified himself and said it was urgent he talk with Detective Sergeant Harold Smith.

Boone turned slightly and stared at a glass wall while he waited to be connected with Harker.

I listened to Boone's half of the conversation. At one point he said, "Yes, part of a pool cue."

The Sacramento detective must have said positive things about me, because Boone's demeanor changed significantly after he thanked Smith and placed his receiver on his desk phone.

I assumed the young chief considered me a suspect until Harker vouched for me. After their conversation I became his ally for about ten minutes. By the end of that time Boone must have concluded I had very little to offer to help him solve the first Lincoln City murder since the town council hired him as chief four years earlier.

Then, instead of a person of interest, I became a name in a report.

Sergeant Sutter drove me back to the RV resort. I opened my trailer, called Penny outside, and, while she sniffed, I fetched my phone and tapped the Kings' number.

William King answered.

"This is Dan Ballantine," I said. "I apologize for the late call, but Michael Thomas was murdered outside his home earlier this evening a short time after I talked with him."

"He was?"

"Yes. I spent the last forty minutes in Lincoln City Police Chief Andrew Boone's office answering his questions and learning someone put a bullet in Thomas' brain.

"Please be wary, Bill," I said. "I believe the killer is headed your way."

"He may be headed for Tacoma, Dan, but we aren't there," said King. "Bella and I got approved for vacation time off last Monday and left the next day for Sacramento to visit Bella's parents."

"That's good, Bill," I said. "Enjoy your stay."

"Thanks for calling, Dan."

33—Mosul, January, 2005

"You guys know I'm getting short, right?" asked Sergeant Goldman.

"You haven't said anything," said Sam.

"Short for going back to the World or have you been trimming your dick?" asked Tuck.

"Short for going back to the World *and* for completing my six year enlistment," said the NCO.

"How long?" asked Sam.

"Three months here in Hell and two more back at Fort Lewis after that."

"Not quite a two-digit midget," said Sam.

"That's why Sergeant Villahermosa has been sniffing around our Stryker like a fucking dog in heat," said Tuck. "He wants the credit for your re-enlistment. Are you going to wait until you're back at Fort Lewis or let him have the bennies?"

The three soldiers sat in the shade on the west side of their Stryker. They had survived the depression of the Christmas season away from home and waited for a call to action.

"I'm thinking about *not* giving *any* re-enlistment N C O any bennies," said Goldman. "I may have considered a career in This Man's Army once upon a time, but I can't see doing it another fourteen years."

"What will you do on the outside?" asked Sam.

"Go to college."

"You looking to make a comeback as a civilian?" asked Tuck.

Goldman looked at the specialist. "You can't have a comeback if you've never been any-fucking-place."

"What will you study?" asked Sam.

"Fuck if I know," said Goldman. "Something fucking easy. History maybe. I mainly want to use up those education bennies the recruitment N C O kept telling me about."

"Which college?" asked Sam.

"It can't be in Southern fucking California 'cause that puts me way too close to my mother and her rabbi," said Goldman. "Believe me when I say I spent enough fucking hours in temple to last two lifetimes."

"If not close to Mom then where?" asked Sam.

"I was thinking Humboldt State 'cause they've got the best grass up there," said Goldman. "But I'll need to work part time to make ends meet, so I guess I'll apply to Sacramento State instead."

34

Penny and I walked the short path to the Pacific Ocean Monday morning. A breeze whipped a spray off the waves and cooled us on a sunny day as we walked along the short. I read once that nine out every ten living things live in the ocean, but I had trouble believing that ratio. If they counted every plankton, did they also count every ant?

While Penny sniffed, I thought about the former Sigma Pis. I had warned Breckinridge, Thomas, and King, and the first two were dead anyway. Though Bill King had left his home, I assumed he would return at some point in time.

I assumed the killer had watched the Thomas residence and waited for Michael's return and would do the same with King. He appeared to be a patient man driven by his desire to murder every Sigma Pi fraternity brother involved with Joshua Goldman's death.

Bill and Bella King would return home some time.

Penny led me along the vacant beach while I wondered what I could do about the situation.

Once upon a time a man watching a flying Frisbee said, "I wondered why the Frisbee was getting bigger, and then it hit me."

I called Bill King and asked, "How would you like a house sitter?"

"I don't understand, Dan," said King.

"I believe the man who killed Michael Thomas watched his home several days waiting for Thomas to return from a vacation," I said. "As far as I know, the killer did not have any idea when Thomas would return. But his research must have told him Thomas had not moved recently, and he watched and waited patiently."

"And you think he may do the same thing at our house in Tacoma?"

"I do," I said. "I've been thinking about these killings as I've traveled. I think the killer knows what his targets looked like six years ago. He may have secured a copy of the Sigma Pi yearbook for that year. Mario Martinelli told me it would have had all the members' photos in it."

"It did," said Bill. "I still have mine."

"Well, you probably haven't changed all that much," I said, "and I doubt the killer would confuse me for you. But I am willing to wait in your home and watch for strangers watching for you. There's a chance I'll see him before he sees you."

"I suppose that's possible," said Bill.

I heard doubt in his voice.

"Detective Smith and I believe the killer somehow manages to appear non-threatening," I said. "He managed to get Jeff Sanford's consent to enter the Sanford home and murder Jeff Sanford just inside the door.

"He also obtained consent to enter Tyler Thompson's apartment and murdered Thompson while sitting next to him on his couch. I believe he talked with Curt Hendricks outside a bar and said words which kept Curt outside and lured him to a beach parking lot where he shot him in the face and walked away unseen.

"He made an appointment with Truman Breckinridge for a lawn replacement estimate and murdered him just inside the door of an empty home which Breckinridge entered voluntarily notwithstanding the fact I had warned him to watch out for a man with a gun.

"And, finally, he approached Michael Thomas while Thomas walked his dog on a public street just after sunset and shot both him and his dog."

"He must be using a quiet gun," said Bill.

"He shoots twenty-two shorts which are probably the quietest round available to the public," I said. "He may also use a suppressor, a silencer. Instructions for how to make them are available on the internet."

"But if he knows what I look like, he's not going to approach you, Dan," said Bill.

"Not if he sees me, but I could wait in your house and photograph every person who comes to your door the instant I open it."

Bill did not speak.

After several dead seconds I said, "Frankly, Bill, there's not much we know about this guy except he wants to kill you. If he wants to put a small bullet through your right eye like he has all the others, he has to get close to you. I'm willing to sit in your house while you're gone. If you're not comfortable with that, I'll bid you good luck and go fishing."

"House sitting for Bella and me is not my concern, Dan," said Bill. "I guess I was hoping the killer would get tired of waiting for us to come home and give up. We told our neighbor Bella's mother was gravely ill, and we would be away indefinitely.

"If you're there in our house, the killer will know we're coming home some time relatively soon."

"That's true," I said, "but it wouldn't take much time on the World Wide Web to find you still own the house and still pay taxes and utility bills on it. That information can easily be found in public records.

"But, hey, it's your call," I said. "I feel better for making the offer. Good luck to you and Bella, Bill. Sorry I bothered you again."

"Wait, Dan," said Bill. "First, it's no bother. Second, Bella and I appreciate your concern.

"Let me sound your idea off Bella and call you back in a few minutes. Okay?"

"Okay, Bill," I said. "I'll be leaving Lincoln City in an hour or so. Please call within that time if possible."

"I will, Dan, and thanks again."

King called, told me his retired neighbor had a house key, and wished me luck. He also told me he had called the neighbor who had agreed to maintain their yard in their absence, advised him I would be house sitting, and gave him an estimated return date a week away.

As I retraced my route to Gig Harbor, I stopped at the Evergreen Aviation and Space Museum in McMinnville and walked around Howard Hughes' Spruce Goose. I also enjoyed the other planes exhibited there.

I reached the Gig Harbor RV resort an hour before sun down, dropped my trailer, and took Penny and three days of food and clothing to the Kings' house in my Jimmy. After obtaining a house key from the nosey neighbor, I found the garage door switch, opened the door, and moved my truck inside out of sight. With my flashlight I verified a fence enclosed the Kings' back yard so I could let Penny do her toilet business without showing either of us at the front of the house.

I called Bill King and advised him I was on duty inside his home. I promised to call each evening with a report.

Before noon the next day I felt like a prisoner and, as I sat with a Vince Flynn novel in the Kings' living room, I questioned my plan to spot the killer.

While driving from Las Vegas toward Lincoln City, I had reached a conclusion that had jumped into my mind every day since: the killer may have been watching the Breckinridge home when I visited Truman that Friday evening. If so, he saw me and my Jimmy.

That possibility did not stop me from visiting the Thomas residence twice, but if the patient killer had also been watching the Thomas home, he must be thinking about the coincidence of me appearing at two of his targets' homes.

In *Goldfinger,* Ian Fleming had evil Auric Goldfinger tell his hero, "Mister Bond, they have a saying in Chicago: 'The first time is happenstance; the second time is coincidence; the third time, it's enemy action.'"

If the killer was watching the Kings' residence when I arrived, he had probably seen me for the third time and might consider me an enemy. I doubted he would add me to his murder list, but he had time on his side. He could wait and watch until the Kings returned home, I left, and Bill and Bella resumed their daily routines.

I decided my trips to and from my trailer and the grocery store would be made at one o'clock in the morning. The killer had to sleep some time, and I doubted he would nap during the day.

If the Kings' doorbell worked, I could sleep anytime I felt like it.

I am not particularly curious how others live, but I was happy to discover the Kings kept a clean and tidy home. I might have withdrawn my offer to house sit had I found mold growing on dirty dishes in a sink or ants feasting on dropped crumbs.

The small house had three bedrooms: the master bedroom, a guest room with a double bed, and an office with two desks. Each desk held a computer and flat screen monitor. A scanner and printer occupied a small table which sat between the desks next to a four-drawer file cabinet.

A hallway held a pair of matching bookcases stuffed with hardbacks, paperbacks, and magazines. The reading material ranged from mysteries and thrillers to self-help and travel.

Family photographs and nature photos and prints decorated the walls. From the number of people in various shots, I guessed Bella came from a large family and Bill a smaller one.

A fifty-inch flat screen television had been bolted to one living room wall, and the cabinet below it contained an eclectic collection of DVDs in what appeared, at first, to be a random order.

The Kings alphabetized the files in their office cabinet, but I discovered the DVDs were separated by genre. Thrillers and action movies occupied the right half of the cabinet; love stories and vampire flicks the left.

Or else Bill took one side, and Bella the other.

My father told me he began to build what he hoped would be an extensive collection of westerns on VHS tapes when those devices became popular before my birth. Two years and forty movies later Lansing realized he had only watched three films, *Jeremiah Johnson, The Magnificent Seven,* and *The Professionals* more than once.

Lansing stopped collecting and, when DVDs replaced VHS tapes, he only replaced those same three favorites.

Bill King not only had those three, he had what looked like every western John Wayne and Randolph Scott ever made. He also had television episodes from *Wanted Dead or Alive, Gunsmoke, The Virginian, Have Gun—Will Travel, Lonesome Dove, Deadwood,* and many more including Dad's favorite, *Lawman,* which starred John Russell as Marshal Dan Troop.

Lansing named me after Marshal Dan Troop, and I may have disappointed him by not becoming a U S Marshal. Earning an LAPD uniform may not have been lawman enough to make Dad happy, but he never said anything to me about it.

When I tired of reading, I watched *Lonesome Dove.* I had seen parts of it with Lansing, and I found myself fast forwarding through the sections which did not involve Gus and Call and the cowboys driving the herd.

During my third and fourth days in the King home I watched the first season of *Dexter*. The serial killer who works in a police department where his sister works as a detective fascinated me. The show reinforced my belief some bad guys are getting away with their crimes.

I wondered if the killer of Jeff Sanford, Tyler Thompson, Curt Hendricks, Truman Breckinridge, Michael Thomas, and, presumably, William King, would get away with it.

I calculated he had a good chance.

35

The killer watched the GMC truck pull into the Kings' drive and the tall man get out and walk with his leashed dog to the neighbor's house. After the tall man returned and moved the GMC into the Kings' garage, the killer did not see him or the dog again until the Kings arrived at four in the afternoon eight days later.

Through his telescope the killer watched the tall man back his GMC from the garage so Bill King could park his Explorer inside. When the GMC backed into the street, the killer could see the tall man's dog in the front passenger seat.

The killer followed the GMC to Gig Harbor, and, when it turned into the RV resort, continued to a gas station, reversed direction, and returned to the Kings' residence.

Fifteen minutes after the killer returned, parked, moved to the back of the minivan, and resumed a long-distance watch, Bella King backed the Explorer from the garage and drove away.

The killer waited ten minutes then donned a white jumpsuit. With a small tool box in a naked right hand, the killer walked half a block to the Kings' side door and knocked.

A second before the door opened, the killer heard Bill King say, "Did you forget … ."

Those were his last words.

The killer pulled a revolver from a left front pocket and shot Bill King through his right eye. As Bill fell, the killer pushed into the house and closed the door.

The killer gloved, forced a section of pool cue into Bill's right eye, and wiped the doorknob before stepping outside. There the killer ungloved and walked to the minivan parked at the end of the street.

36

The sunny afternoon gave me a chance to grill my first semi-fresh fish in nearly two weeks. My definition of 'fresh' means I caught it a few hours before cooking it. Semi-fresh is when somebody else tells me it was caught within the previous twenty-four hours.

The man behind the fish market counter had assured me the ling cod fillet I selected had been caught early that morning.

My mouth watered as I dumped glowing briquets from my heating chimney onto my portable grill's grate. I spread them and dropped the grill in place above them. While it heated, I stepped into my trailer and fetched the cod and a Corona.

I had cooked for myself in the Kings' kitchen while I occupied their home, but I did not use the broiler because I did not want to clean it. When Bill advised me they were headed home and expected to arrive mid-afternoon, I spent the morning putting the house back in order.

During my house sitting days I opened the door to three visitors. A ten-year-old boy wanted me to buy magazines so he could go to basketball camp. A lad a few years older wanted to mow the lawn. And a young couple wanted to tell me about Jesus.

The bible-thumpers could have been a murderous pair, but they did nothing other than register surprise when I raised my digital camera and took their photo.

They left quickly when I told them I was hoping to get a picture of the person who wanted to murder Mister King.

A cool bay breeze let my RVing neighbors share the wonderful smell of my grilling fish, but I did not see any of them watch me while I sat at my picnic table and shared bites with Penny.

An hour later I sat in my favorite camp chair holding my second bottle of Corona and watching the daylight fade. Penny slept on the grass beside me.

An attractive young woman walking along the resort road caught my eyes. She had a small purse over her right shoulder and a plastic grocery store bag in her right hand.

Lansing told me the City of Davis had considered an ordinance requiring local businesses to charge twenty-five cents per bag for those citizens so uncaring about the environment they declined to bring bags of their own.

"Nice," I said softly to nobody in particular.

Penny awakened at the sound of my voice. When she heard footsteps, she got to her feet and put her eyes on the dark-haired beauty.

"Handsome dog," said the young woman. She stopped and asked, "Is she friendly?"

At least she didn't say 'cute,' I thought as I got to my feet.

I enjoy conversing with attractive women of all ages, and I especially like those that like my dog.

"Yes. Her name is Penny."

The young woman said, "Hey, Penny."

Penny trotted to her and permitted herself to be petted and scratched.

That's when I saw a wedding band on the woman's ring finger and whatever hopeful thoughts I might have considered vaporized even as they formed.

The woman looked at me and smiled. "My husband and I are getting by in a small Class C, but we get tired of unhooking the land lines every time we want to go some place. How do you like your fifth-wheel?"

"It's the way to go as far as I'm concerned," I said. "I had a Class C a few years back, and I much prefer leaving the trailer in place while I visit the local sights or go out for a bite I didn't cook myself."

The young woman continued to scratch and pet Penny. "That looks like a fancy one."

"I got a good deal on it last winter from a family that had stopped using it and got tired of paying storage fees," I said. "When I started looking, I found several nice units for sale. People buy them thinking they will use them every weekend, and then they don't. In this crummy economy it seems they are quicker to put them up for sale than keep them."

She nodded. "Any chance I could have a peek at the inside?"

"Sure," I said. I set my bottle on the picnic table and said, "Come, Penny. Let's go inside a minute."

I stepped to my trailer door and opened it. Penny hopped the steps, and the young woman followed her into my living room.

Much like the guy watching the flying Frisbee, when she turned and I saw her hand coming out the shopping bag holding something shiny, it hit me.

My right hand grabbed for the butt of my Smith & Wesson as her left hand brought a stubby twenty-two revolver with a black, sausage-sized suppressor on the muzzle out of the bag.

It seemed like her pistol moved in slow motion as it came up at the end of her outstretched arm to aim at my face.

I fired my forty-four from the hip a split second after I saw a flash of light in the center of the suppressor.

I felt a bite in my right ear as I watched her move backwards and crash to the floor against my sofa.

I stepped to her and planted my right boot on her left hand and gun.

She looked up at me with surprise on her face. Then she raised her head enough to see the blood flowing copiously from two holes an inch apart in the center of her chest. Pain closed her eyes and clenched her teeth.

I stared at her two full minutes. Then the flowing blood slowed to a trickle, her body relaxed, and her last breath huffed past her lips.

I kicked her pistol away from her hand and brought my left hand to my right ear. When I lowered it and looked at it, I saw my own blood.

While Penny sniffed the corpse, I found my phone and tapped the usual numbers. Then I stepped to my bath, reached in and grabbed a white washcloth, and sacrificed it on my wound.

I looked back at my curious dog and the dead girl. "Well, Penny, they can't blame this one on the Y chromosome."

37

"Her full name was Samantha Abawimideh Goldman," I said. "She was Joshua's wife although their marriage was short-lived."

Detective Sergeant Harker Smith and I sat in our favorite booth in the Black Bear Diner. I had called him with a preliminary report when the Gig Harbor police finished with me the evening I shot Samantha. I had promised to meet him for coffee and a more detailed report when I passed through Davis.

"The local cops found her Honda Odyssey parked in a guest space at the R V resort," I said. "It looked like she'd been living out of it for several weeks. A cardboard box contained her laptop, a Sacramento Sigma Pi yearbook from six years ago with photos of six young men circled, and several important documents including a Certificate of Marriage. The laptop had a file which contained a written journal she started after she finished Army basic training.

"She met Goldman when she was assigned to his Stryker vehicle in Mosul, Iraq, in two thousand and four. They fell in love, but, according to her diary, both of them realized nothing could ever come of it because he was Jewish and she was Syrian."

"But they married anyway," said Harker.

"They did," I said, "in Reno on the Tuesday before Goldman died."

"They were honeymooning in Sacra-tomato?" asked Harker.

"As much as a young couple in love can," I said. "Samantha had flown down from Fort Lewis to spend a two week Army leave with Joshua. She had orders sending her to Afghanistan after the leave.

"After a few days they drove to Reno and married. Perhaps visiting the Overtime saloon was part of their celebration. Anyway, after Goldman died, Samantha must have cleaned his apartment, locked it, and returned to Fort Lewis. She completed her active duty commitment to Uncle Sam three days after Jeff Sanford's release from Folsom.

"Her journal included notes that she had made from *Sacramento Bee* articles describing the Overtime brawl, Goldman's death, Sanford's court hearings, and Sanford's release," I said. "The cops told me she had written about 'meeting,' her word, the other Sigmas many times after Joshua died. She had kept notes of her internet searches for them."

"So she planned their murders during the entire time Sanford was in prison," said Harker.

I nodded and sipped coffee. "When Samantha separated from active duty, the Army gave her a plane ticket to her Detroit home. A Gig Harbor detective told me they assumed that's where she bought the twenty-two revolver and the suppressor. The pistol without the suppressor had been stolen in a home burglary two months before Samantha went home.

"Then she withdrew her savings from her bank and took a bus to Sacramento where she paid cash to buy a used Honda Odyssey from a private party. The cops found a receipt for the dark tinting she had done to the rear windows dated two days before she killed Sanford."

"I wonder why it took her so long to kill Thompson."

"We'll never know, but she got them all," I said. "An hour or so after I left the Kings in their Tacoma home,

Bella went grocery shopping. It appears Samantha walked unseen to their back door, knocked, and dropped Bill when he opened it.

"Then she came after me. The cops found a list in her car with Bill's name and all the others crossed off."

"Was your name on her list?"

"No," I said, "but I don't think she ever learned it. I was mentioned as 'the tall man in the GMC' on her list and in her journal. She had seen me in Las Vegas, Lincoln City, and at the Kings' house in Tacoma. She wrote she did not know who I was or why I was involved, but she decided to 'meet' me anyway in case I was a cop.

"That was her term," I added. "'Meet.'"

"By her definition of that term, it looks like she almost did," said Harker. He looked at the bandage on my right ear.

"The E R doctor told me I have a small half moon notch in the outer loop. While he cleaned and bandaged it, he said a plastic surgeon could smooth it for me.

"I wish she had tried to put a bullet in my heart instead of my eye," I said. "I was wearing my light vest as I usually do when I'm working a case. It would have easily stopped a twenty-two short. Instead of a small bruise, I'll have a notch in my ear the rest of my life."

"She was in a rut of shooting bullets into right eyes," said Harker with a smile, "and she aimed for yours out of habit."

"The only difference between a rut and a grave is the depth," I said.

"A lesson lost on her," said Harker.

"She would have ended up just as dead if she had shot me in the chest instead of bringing her twenty-two all the way up to aim at my face."

Harker sipped coffee and nodded.

"I've decided her sex and her cuteness was what allowed her to kill all those Sigma Pis so easily," I said.

"She was an attractive young female. All she had to do was smile, and she would get a rise out of any normal male.

"I will confess to you, Harker, and you only, that my suspicion was not, I repeat, was not sparked while she got friendly with Penny and me and asked to see the inside of my trailer. She was smooth and friendly, and I couldn't help wanting to be friendly and helpful."

"Oh, sure, Dan," said Harker. "You tall, handsome guys get that all the time from foxy babes. A short, homely cop like me would have put his guard up the instant the babe smiled. That simply never happens to guys like me."

"I think 'cop' is the important word there, Harker," I said. "Any guy, married or otherwise, would … ."

"Okay. Okay. What put you on to her?"

"Her gun," I said. "I went into reaction mode when I saw she had a gun in her hand."

Harker smiled. "Like any normal male, right?"

I met his smile. "Well, any normal current or ex-cop.

"She had her back to me while she stepped up into my trailer. When she turned to face me she was pulling her left hand from her shopping bag. When I saw shiny metal in her hand, I grabbed for my Smith."

"Good thing you had it on you."

"I always do," I said. "Even so, she shot me before I shot her.

"If I hadn't leaned a bit to my left as I pulled my Smith from my right hip pocket, she might have stopped my draw when her tiny bullet scrambled my brain.

"While replaying her actions in my mind during my drive down here I decided she made a mistake. Perhaps a fatal mistake."

"What's that?"

"She should have removed her wedding ring and not mentioned her husband when she approached me. My mind abandoned a certain 'normal male' path," I put the words 'normal male' in air quotes, "when I saw the gold band and heard her mention a husband.

"I've concluded mentioning a husband or boyfriend is female-speak for 'don't even think about it.'"

"I've often heard those words my own self," said Harker with a smile. "Maybe she took off her ring for Sanford, Thompson, and Hendricks who she knew were single, but she was such in a hurry to shoot you and get out of Dodge she forgot about it."

"Whatever she was thinking died with her," I said. "Her journal made it easy for the Gig Harbor and Tacoma cops. It will also save you and the cops in Huntington Beach and Las Vegas a bunch of investigation time."

Harker nodded. "Have you told your lady friend you found her brother's shooter?"

"No," I said. "I told Kyra about killing a bad guy once, and I got the feeling she did not approve of that violence even though it was self-defense. You can pass the word to Sanford's and Thompson's people, but I don't know yet how I will tell Kyra I killed a woman."

"I requested hard, certified copies of the Lincoln City, Tacoma, and Gig Harbor police reports for my file," said Harker. "I could mail copies to your Reno P O box, and you could pick the right time and place to show them to her. Maybe if she read about the shooting rather than heard you tell it … ."

I sipped coffee. "That's a good idea, Harker. I'll go fishing for a few days then make a date with her for a week from tomorrow night. By then you'll have sent me those reports. I can let her read them in her condo after dinner. Learning I'm a woman killer may ruin my chances of making it to her bedroom that evening, but if she reads Samantha murdered Michael Thomas and Bill King then immediately came after me, she may accept my shooting Samantha in self-defense a bit easier."

Harker grinned. "Hey, Dan, she might be turned on by the big, strong, straight shooting man with a visible battle scar who avenged her brother's death."

I shook my head. "I doubt it."

Harker finished his coffee.

"Will you advise the Huntington Beach and Las Vegas police departments of what happened?" I asked.

"I'll send them emails with my report attached, but they can print their own copies if they want them," said Harker. "We're watching every penny these days. Even fax pennies."

"I'll pay for the coffee, Harker," I said with a smile.

About The Author.

Mark Travis did law over three decades as a California criminal prosecutor. He wrote novels while waiting his turn at the bar. *INTENT TO DEFRAUD* won the Dark Oak Mystery Contest and publication in 2005.

A HURT FOR A HURT is the ninth story in the Dan Ballantine series.

From his Reno home base Mark travels the west in his motorhome with his dog, Samantha, writing and fishing.

For more information, visit his website: www.marktravisbooks.com.

CPSIA information can be obtained at www.ICGtesting.com
Printed in the USA
BVOW020716050712

294397BV00001B/140/P